Then

The mud sliding toward her, the out of focus face, the skull, and finally the skeletons—this time more vivid than any of the previous assaults on her senses. A cold shudder moved up her spine, followed by a lump in her throat and a churning in the pit of her stomach. She hugged her shoulders in an attempt to fend off the shivers, but not from the cold. Her insides trembled to the point where she felt as if she had no control over her own body. Even though she still didn't understand the message trying to get through to her, this time the vision truly frightened her on both a physical and emotional level.

This time it felt very real...and very personal.

She tried to shake off the uncomfortable feelings, but without much success. Then a new sensation hit her, an eerie awareness of someone watching her. Someone obscured by the fog. Someone laying in wait. Someone wanting to harm her? The possibility sent a hard jolt of fear racing through her veins. It played on her already tautly stretched nerves. A genuine sense of alarm welled inside her. She fought the desire to run blindly down the road. But toward what? And away from whom? One thing loomed abundantly clear...she needed to move on, to get away from this spot that radiated a feeling bordering on evil.

Lexi hurried down the road toward the mansion as she fought against the almost uncontrollable urge to continually glance over her shoulder. The panic built, layer upon layer. The danger close on her heels, almost as if it could reach out and grab her.

Praise for *Déjà Vu*'s Author

Samantha Gentry has received excellent reviews for her romance novels:

UNEXPECTED ENCOUNTER

STEAMY ENCOUNTER

MASKED ENCOUNTER

All are available from the Scarlet Rose line of The Wild Rose Press.

Déjà Vu

by

Samantha Gentry

Best Regards,

Samantha Gentry

This is a work of fiction. Names, characters, places, and incidents are either the product of the author's imagination or are used fictitiously, and any resemblance to actual persons living or dead, business establishments, events, or locales, is entirely coincidental.

Déjà Vu

COPYRIGHT © 2009 by Samantha Gentry

All rights reserved. No part of this book may be used or reproduced in any manner whatsoever without written permission of the author or The Wild Rose Press except in the case of brief quotations embodied in critical articles or reviews.
Contact Information: info@thewildrosepress.com

Cover Art by *Kim Mendoza*

The Wild Rose Press
PO Box 706
Adams Basin, NY 14410-0706
Visit us at www.thewildrosepress.com

Publishing History
First Crimson Rose Edition, 2010
Print ISBN 1-60154-616-5

Published in the United States of America

Chapter One

Alexandra Caldwell shivered, hunching her shoulders against the stiff ocean breeze as the boat pulled up to the dock at Skull Island. Even the name left her uneasy...*Skull Island*. It sounded like a sinister place inhabited by pirates, thugs, and other undesirables.

She glanced up at the angry storm clouds darkening the sky to the point where it seemed more like evening than eleven o'clock in the morning. Another tremor of apprehension washed through her body. Ever since she was a little girl, thunder and lightning had frightened her. But as much as she wanted to blame the approaching storm for her uneasiness, it wasn't solely responsible.

She forced her attention to the tall man standing dockside as he grabbed the line thrown to him and secured the vessel. He extended his hand to help her out of the boat. The instant they made physical contact, a potent arc of energy raced through her body followed by a moment of panic. The hair on her arms stood on end. Her mouth went dry and her throat tried to close.

The vision exploded in her mind. Mud...a wall of mud sliding down an embankment toward her. A fleeting glance of an out-of-focus face that turned into a human skull. Then a skeleton. And a second skeleton. She jerked her hand from his grasp while trying to force a calm to her momentary panic.

She didn't know how to control her psychic abilities and didn't always understand what the strange images, feelings, and dreams meant. However, she did know when they tried to tell her something important and this was definitely one of those times.

The man cocked his head to one side. A slight frown wrinkled across his brow as he stared at her with a quizzical expression. "Is something wrong? You look like you've seen a ghost."

She quickly recovered her composure, at least outwardly, and extended a businesslike smile. "No, nothing is wrong. Just a little spark of static electricity, I guess. It must have something to do with..." she glanced up at the threatening sky as a shiver of anxiety swept through her. "...uh, this approaching storm."

She returned her attention to the man, her demeanor all business. "I'm Alexandra Caldwell. Mr. Talbot is expecting me."

"I'm Gable Talbot."

"You're Gable Talbot?" She couldn't hide her surprise. This man whose touch had sparked a disturbing sequence of frightening images was not at all what she had anticipated the owner of Skull Island would look like. He had to be six-one, maybe even six-foot-two inches tall with broad shoulders, long legs, and an athletic build. He was also much younger than she thought he would be. He appeared to be in his late thirties. Soft looking sable brown hair framed his ruggedly handsome chiseled features. And his eyes—she had never seen such intense green eyes. They could almost be called mesmerizing. No doubt about it, he definitely qualified as president of the Drop Dead Gorgeous Hunk Club.

"Here's her luggage, Mr. Talbot." The deck hand's voice interrupted her thoughts. "I've also got some mail for you, a delivery for Dolly from that catalogue company, and this package that architect fellow has been waiting for." He emitted a soft chuckle. "Looks like it got here just in time for him to get it before he leaves."

"Thanks, Jimmy." A teasing grin spread across Gable's face revealing a row of perfect white teeth. "Better it should arrive *before* he leaves rather than after."

"I also had two of those reporters wanting me to bring them here. I did like you said and told them no one gets on the island unless you've approved them. They tried to tell me you said it was okay, but I told them I had to hear it directly from you. Then they offered me more money." A spontaneous laugh escaped his throat. "I told them I'd be glad to take their money…as soon as you gave the okay."

"You did the right thing." A scowl covered Gable's face as he muttered under his breath. "Damn reporters. If I'd known my announcement was going to cause such an uproar, I would have found another way of doing it."

"What do you want me to do about the barge? If we're going to bring over heavy construction equipment, I need to get it on the schedule."

"I'll let you know about that in a few days."

"Sure thing, Mr. Talbot."

Gable cast off the line, looking up at the angry storm clouds as the boat pulled away from the dock. He returned his attention to the woman who had invaded his island. "It's going to be raining any minute now. We'd better get up to the house." He quickly loaded everything on the back of the electric cart, and they started up the road.

He glanced at her as he cleared his mind of the troubling thoughts about the reporters, choosing instead to focus on her physical appearance. She was tall for a woman, probably five-foot-eight—a perfect match for his six-two frame. She appeared to be in her early-to-mid thirties. Her short, wind-blown hair was ash blond, her eyes a bright hazel surrounded by long, dark lashes. Her delicately sculpted features presented one of the most beautiful and alluring faces he had ever seen, one that triggered thoughts of carefree days and passion filled nights. He made note of the absence of a wedding ring or even an engagement ring, usually the first thing he checked when meeting an attractive woman.

She presented a desirable package—in fact, *very* desirable. A momentary tightness pulled across his chest confirming just how much he was attracted to her. Clenching his jaw into a hard line of determination, he reminded himself that he didn't have time to pursue a beautiful woman right now, regardless of how much she sparked his libido. Perhaps if the circumstances had been different, if he didn't already have a critical agenda that took precedence over everything else.

"I must be honest with you, Miss Caldwell—"

"Please, call me Lexi."

"Okay...Lexi." Something about her voice penetrated his hastily constructed wall of resistance, a throaty quality that sounded very sexy yet natural rather than put on. It truly matched the way she looked. Once again, he shoved aside his momentary mental detour and turned his attention to his primary objective.

"I'm having second thoughts about allowing you to do research here on Skull Island for one of J.D. Prescott's books. I've read a couple of his novels and I don't see how researching a thirty-year-old true life missing person case fits in with the type of books he writes. We're talking about a situation where two people disappeared, a big name newspaper publisher and his wife. Their bodies were never found. In fact, they couldn't even find evidence of foul play even though logic said the missing couple didn't walk out the door hand-in-hand and disappear into thin air of their own volition. As far as I know, there isn't even an ongoing investigation into the case. It's old news, what you could call a very cold case. J.D. Prescott writes horror stories. I'm not seeing the connection."

He paused, making sure his attitude and voice didn't in any way project what was really going on inside him. "I also don't see why it's necessary for you to do this research here on the island. I'm sure all the information you need could be located in the newspaper archives, at the sheriff's office, and on the internet. There couldn't possibly be anything physical here that would relate to what happened thirty years ago. Anything considered evidence at that time would have been collected by the sheriff's department during the original investigation."

Lexi flashed a confident smile. "I appreciate your cooperation, Mr. Talbot—"

"Gable."

"Gable...it will be helpful to me if I can get the feel of the island. See the Victorian mansion where the party was held that night, retrace the footsteps of the guests present at the party, immerse myself in the setting—that type of thing. Mr. Prescott has also requested photographs of the island as it is now to compare to photos of the way things looked thirty years ago. He wants pictures of the areas where you plan to do any construction and major landscaping such as the location of the golf course, new buildings, and the small plane landing strip."

She paused for a moment as if trying to gather the proper words. "And it wasn't two people who disappeared. It was three."

Shock jolted through Gable's body shoving his senses on full alert. No one had bothered to mention the third person in many years. It was almost as if he hadn't existed beyond the original investigation and the surrounding lurid gossip. After a couple of years any mention in the news of the disappearances only dealt with the high profile Winthrop Hollingsworth and his wife, Evelyn, but not the third person.

Not Jack Stinson.

He tried to regain his composure as he forced a casualness to his voice that he didn't feel. How deeply had she delved into the history? Did she know more than she should? *"Three* people? I thought we were talking about Winthrop and Evelyn Hollingsworth. If what I heard from the previous owners of the island is correct, they disappeared about a year after Winthrop inherited the entire Hollingsworth newspaper publishing empire, including this island." Even to his own ear, his voice did not sound as convincing as he would have liked. "That made him one of the wealthiest men in the country at the age of only thirty-five."

"Skull Island is such an...uh...*unusual* name. Do you know how that came about?"

She had abruptly changed the subject. His mind raced in an attempt to figure out the reason...or perhaps it was nothing more than simple curiosity on her part. Exactly what were her true intentions? Or more specifically, J.D. Prescott's true intentions. Or maybe his own hidden agenda had him jumping to conclusions, making something significant out of an innocent question. He tried to rein in his trepidation and deal with her question as if it didn't mean anything more than what it appeared on the surface.

"It's the shape of the island. From the air you can see that the shoreline bears a resemblance to a human skull with two of the wooded areas where eyes would be. I don't know who actually decided on that for a name, whether it was the Hollingsworth family when they originally purchased the island in 1919 or someone who owned it before them."

"Hmm...perhaps some old maps of the area

might indicate when it was named Skull Island or if it had another name at one time. Maybe I could find the information if I did a real estate title search."

Gable nervously cleared his throat as he attempted to get her back to the topic that had grabbed his attention. "This third person you mentioned, that's something I hadn't heard about."

"The third person was a man named Jack Stinson. He worked for Winthrop Hollingsworth. The *official* theory at the time said Evelyn Hollingsworth and Jack Stinson were having an affair. He wanted her to leave her husband. When she refused, he murdered Winthrop. The story goes that Evelyn was horrified at what he had done and refused to go with him. So, to protect himself, he murdered her, too. Gossip had Jack Stinson changing his name and slipping out of the country before the sheriff could take him into custody. After all, Canada is very close to this location. Only a few miles from here once you're back on the Washington state mainland.

"Several theories existed as to why the bodies were never found, all of them speculation without any evidence. At the time of the investigation, a member of the island household staff confirmed to a sheriff's deputy that a small motor boat went missing that night. The sheriff believed Jack Stinson escaped using that boat and dumped the bodies in the ocean somewhere between the island and the mainland."

"Well, that's an interesting theory, but what do *you* think? What has your research led you to believe?"

Lexi glanced at him. He stared straight ahead at the road as he drove the cart, but the set of his jaw and the intensity that covered his features told her it was more than a casual question. She needed to be cautious in what she said, but she wasn't too sure why that decision had popped into her head.

She carefully measured her words before speaking. "I haven't formed an opinion. I'm a researcher, not an investigative reporter or a detective. I've been hired to gather research information for an author, not investigate a thirty-year-old mystery with the hope of solving it. My job isn't a matter of why it happened or to hunt for new clues to solve a cold case. It's to collect accurate information for someone else's use rather than draw conclusions or form theories."

"Doesn't your curiosity ever lead you down a path of new discovery when doing your research?"

She wrinkled her brow in a bit of a frown as she considered his question. "I do have to admit this is different from the type of research I usually do. Normally I gather facts about a known thing. It could be a specific period in history or an event. Sometimes it's information about a prominent public figure—living or dead—whether a politician or celebrity or scientist. It might be material on a location or even facts about a specific job such as biochemist. That type of thing. I've never researched an unsolved mystery, at least not a contemporary one rather than historical."

She hadn't formulated her thoughts in those exact terms before. This was an unusual research contract that deviated from her regular assignments. It had already produced unexpected results in the form of a tingle of excitement caused by Gable's nearness combined with the anxiety of the psychic vision that had assaulted her senses. A little shiver told her nothing was as it appeared. So, until she could figure out what was going on, she needed to keep her thoughts to herself rather than voice her concerns.

"Well, unless Prescott is weaving a tale that shows the dead bodies rising from the ocean and wreaking havoc on the living, I still don't see how the disappearance thirty years ago connects with the type of books J.D. Prescott writes."

"I'm afraid I can't give you any insight into Mr. Prescott's intentions. He hasn't told me how he plans to use the information." Everything about the conversation sent warning signals telling Lexi to be cautious, that Gable's mention of having second thoughts about her research contained more than was apparent on the surface. It was the type of psychic message she had learned to trust even though she usually didn't understand what the messages meant.

She wanted to put this line of conversation to rest rather than continue what could only turn into some sort of verbal joust. "I've never met J.D. Prescott in person or even spoken with him on the phone. All of our communication has been via email. I'm only a freelance researcher hired to dig into the disappearance as background information, what Mr. Prescott referred to as back story. In addition to all the material from the past, he also wants to know as much as you're willing to reveal about your current plans for turning what has always been a private retreat into a luxury resort. After all, this is the scene of the crime, so to speak, and the mysterious events of that night have never been explained."

Gable slowed the cart to a crawl and pointed to the large Victorian structure set back from the right side of the road. "That's the original mansion house. It will be the central building of the resort complex. As you can see, with its close proximity to the dock it will be very convenient as the registration lobby for arriving guests checking into the resort. In addition to the lobby it will contain a fine dining restaurant, informal cafe, cocktail lounge, spa, gift shop, and some of the guest rooms. There will also be a small marina for those arriving by private boat rather than resort water taxi."

"Is that where you're living now?"

"No, it's not currently in use. The previous owners of the island used it as their vacation home. All the original furnishings are there and it's pretty much the same as when the Hollingsworth family built it in 1920. I've been inside it quite a bit during the last six months due to meetings with the architect about the renovation plans. Hank and Dolly go inside every couple of days or so to make sure everything is okay. The utilities are still on."

"Hank and Dolly?"

"Hank and Dolly Billings. They're the island caretakers, have been for over thirty years. Each time the island is sold, their services seem to be part of the sale. They live in the caretaker's cottage on the other side of the mansion."

"They've been here more than thirty years?"

The way Lexi grabbed the notebook from her purse and jotted down the information told Gable she had read more into what he said than what he meant.

Her questions came rapid fire. "Then they worked here at the time of the disappearance? They were employed by the Hollingsworth family? Haven't you ever discussed the disappearance with them?"

"No, it never came up in conversation."

He mentally kicked himself. *You damn idiot! You couldn't have come up with anything more asinine than that even if you'd tried.* He shouldn't have revealed that much about Hank and Dolly, either. It was something Lexi would be able to easily discover on her own, but it shouldn't have come from him. Her questions were very logical considering the new information he had just handed her. And then for him to have stupidly said *it never came up in conversation*...well, the damage had already been done and there was no way for him to conveniently

Déjà Vu

undo it. No doubt about it. The best way to handle the situation would be to ignore it rather than trying to explain away his colossal screw-up. To do anything else would give his blunder credence by following up on it.

He resumed his speed as he pointed toward the structure on the bluff to the left side of the road. "That's my vacation house. I had it built two years ago along with this road from the dock. It's my private residence and not part of the proposed resort area."

The last thing he needed was for some nosy researcher to become suspicious, to think he knew more than he should—more than someone whose only connection to her research was the fact that he happened to be the current owner of the property. He made a mental note to be cautious about volunteering any information pre-dating his purchase of Skull Island four and a half years ago. And that included talking about Winthrop's grandfather using the island as a base between Canada and the United States for smuggling liquor during Prohibition. The illegal activities amassed another fortune for him on top of the one he already had.

A sudden gust of cold wind rippled across the canvas top of the electric cart. Gable drew in a deep breath. The unmistakable scent of rain filled his lungs. If they didn't hurry, they would be caught in it.

"We need to be—"

A loud clap of thunder exploded around them, sending a sharp jolt of trepidation slicing through Lexi's body. She physically jerked to attention as her muscles tensed. Her heartbeat jumped. She attempted to slow it down by gulping in a couple of deep breaths.

Gable stopped the cart and turned toward her,

genuine concern covering his features. "Are you all right?"

"I'm sorry." She gestured toward the menacing clouds. "It's the storm. Thunder and lightning..." Her voice trailed off as the large raindrops hit against the cart's canopy.

Gable pressed the accelerator all the way down causing the cart to lurch forward. "We're almost to my house."

They drove directly into the garage. He plugged the cart into an electrical outlet so it would be fully charged the next time he used it. Then he grabbed her suitcase and the mail. "Come on. I'll show you to your room."

They entered the house from the garage through a large utility room consisting of laundry facilities as well as storage, then into the kitchen. He led her along a walkway with a glass outer wall that bordered the fully enclosed courtyard connecting to the structure on the other side. Anyone going from the front of the house to the back wing on the other side of the courtyard would not need to go outside and face the elements. He indicated a corner room, then stood aside so she could enter. He followed her, placing her suitcase on the floor next to the large closet.

Lexi's gaze traveled around the tastefully decorated, spacious room with large windows on two sides. She noted the door leading to a private bathroom, a definite luxury for a guest bedroom in a private residence.

She turned to Gable, extending her best smile. "This is very nice. Thank you for allowing me to stay here for a few days. I really appreciate your generosity. I'll try to keep out of your way and not be a bother."

"No problem. Feel free to go where you want. There are walking paths that circle the island and

Déjà Vu

also criss-cross it as well as roads for the electric carts. At this time there aren't any gasoline powered vehicles on the island and my plan is to keep it that way once construction is completed."

Feel free to go where you want may have been his words, but she could see the caution in his eyes that said something entirely different, echoing the words he had spoken earlier about having second thoughts. And again her concerns pushed at her reality. Something was wrong. Things were not as they appeared.

"If you don't mind postponing your unpacking, I'll introduce you to my other guests and give you a tour of the house so you'll know where to find things. Then you can make yourself at home. The doors to the front wing of the house aren't locked, so you can come and go as you please. Once the resort is completed and other people are on the island full time, I'll probably need to lock them. But for now, you and my other guests can enter and exit the house as you wish."

She cocked her head and looked at him questioningly. "You have other guests staying here?"

"For the last couple of days I've been involved in business meetings concerning the resort project. The architect, golf course designer, and contractor are here."

"Then those you just mentioned, Hank and Dolly, and you and I are the only people on the island?"

"There's also security personnel. I had to put on guards to keep trespassers off the island following my announcement of the resort plans which resurrected all the old stories about the disappearances. The tabloid reporters have been particularly aggressive in trying to get on the island." His jaw tightened into a hard line. "They're the ones who made a major event out of a thirty-year-old unsolved disappearance by spreading it all over their front pages."

He turned and stared out the window at what she noted was now a full blown rainstorm. "There are only two ways onto this island, by air and by sea. Since we haven't cleared an area for a runway yet, the only air approach would be with a helicopter. No one can sneak onto the island in a noisy helicopter. As far as the sea approach is concerned, there are only two places where someone could come ashore by boat. One of them is the dock where you arrived and the other is a very small, secluded sandy cove where someone could beach a small boat. The rest of the shoreline is rocky cliffs which aren't compatible with a boat landing, not even a rubber raft, let alone a larger vessel of some sort."

A sudden thought struck Lexi. She stared at Gable as she turned the notion over in her mind. "Could someone gain access to the island at one of the rocky areas from a boat anchored off shore by using scuba gear?"

He laughed, a spontaneous moment that showed a dazzling smile. "That's an interesting story idea. You sound like you're writing J.D. Prescott's book for him." The laugh faded as he established eye contact with her. He cocked his head. "Are you? J.D. Prescott is such a recluse. From what I hear, no one knows what he looks like. Not even a photograph for publicity purposes. Is it possible that he doesn't really exist at all and you are the author?"

The intensity of his stare, the depth of his green eyes, sent a quick tremor of excitement shooting through her. No question about it. He was a dynamic man—very sexy and desirable. She forced a calm to her words. "That's a pretty fanciful notion. Perhaps you're the one who should turn a hand to writing fiction."

His voice dropped to a mere whisper. "Well now,

Déjà Vu

that's not really an answer to my question."

"No, I'm not a writer. If I had written the J.D. Prescott books, I would have needed to write the first one when I was in grade school. I'm only gathering...uh, gathering information." She didn't like the breathless quality that seemed to cling to her words. "It...uh...it seemed to me to be the type of detail about the island's geography that would be helpful to Mr. Prescott."

They remained still, standing almost toe-to-toe, neither of them saying anything. Gable finally broke the nearly trance-like moment when he brushed a loose tendril of hair away from her cheek. The heated intensity sizzled between them for an instant, then he turned toward the door.

"Let's take that tour. I'll introduce you to my other guests." They started back the way they had come. "In this back guest wing, in addition to the six guest rooms, there's a small kitchenette where guests can have early morning coffee or a late night snack. As you can see, the center courtyard has a year round swimming pool along with the adjacent Jacuzzi." They entered the larger front section of the house. He showed her the way to an oversized office where three men were seated at a small conference table.

"This is Fred Turnbull, the architect who designed this house for me. He's also doing the renovations on the mansion and designing the rest of the resort buildings. Next to him is Stuart Brooks, designer of the championship eighteen-hole golf course we'll be building. And last, but certainly not least, is Walter Denning, the contractor for the resort project."

Gable turned toward her. "Gentlemen, this is Alexandra Caldwell. She's the researcher I mentioned to you this morning. She's gathering background information about the Hollingsworth disappearance for a new book by J.D. Prescott. She'll be staying here for a few days."

Lexi smiled. "It's nice to meet you. I'll try to stay out of your way. I know you have business with Mr. Talbot that's certainly more pressing than what I'm doing."

Gable addressed his comments to the men seated at the table. "I'll be right back." He checked his watch. "It's almost lunch time. I'll have Dolly fix something for us and we can eat while we work. I want to complete most of our agenda today so we can easily finish up tomorrow and you'll be able to leave the day after, as scheduled."

He escorted Lexi down the hall, giving her a quick tour of the front section of the house—living room, formal dining room, kitchen with informal eating area, den, a game room containing a pool table and poker table with an archway opening connecting it to the den, and two guest bathrooms. He indicated a room being used as a temporary security office that would ultimately be a library once the resort renovations to the mansion were complete and the security offices moved there along with the business offices.

"I had no idea this house was so large. It didn't appear to be this big as we approached it. Do you live here all year round? It seems so isolated for a full time residence..." She paused as she formulated the words, hoping they sounded casual rather than giving the impression she was prying into his personal life—which was exactly what she was doing. "Especially if you're trying to run a business of some sort."

"I have a condominium in Seattle that's my primary residence. This is a vacation home. After the resort is completed, many full time employees will live on the island in newly constructed employee housing, most of it a dorm type facility with cottages for management personnel."

"What about you? Will you be living here year round after the resort is completed or will your business interests keep you in Seattle?" She caught the way he had ignored her subtle attempt to elicit information. Perhaps the time for subtlety had passed. "If you don't mind me asking, what is it you do for a living? You seem very young to be able to afford to buy an entire island and then the cost of turning it into a resort..." A nervous jitter worked its way through her body. She was every bit as curious about this dynamic and sexy man with his commanding presence as she was about the research information she had been hired to collect.

"Me? It's...family money—inherited. I play golf, travel...things like that. My primary *work* is to oversee my investments."

It immediately hit her. He was suddenly trying too hard to project the image of someone living off the family fortune. Something about it did not ring true. Then the vision invaded her mind again sending a wave of anxiety rippling across her skin— mud sliding down an embankment, coming toward her, trapping her. The same out of focus face, only this time not quite as blurred. The face dissolved into a skull, a skeleton, and a second skeleton.

The words reverberated inside her head as loudly as if someone had actually spoken them. *Everything he just said is a lie. What is he hiding? And why?*

Chapter Two

Gable opened the door to the security office, then stepped aside so Lexi could enter. She hesitated a moment, weighing the options in her mind about how to handle what he had said about inherited family money. She decided to let it drop...for the moment. Then another thought popped into her mind, a startling one. Could he possibly be related to the Hollingsworth family? Could some of the Hollingsworth fortune be the money he inherited? That would certainly put an interesting twist on things. She definitely intended to delve into the background of Gable Talbot before she left Skull Island. The only question being whether her curiosity related to her research or had it been prompted by her undeniable attraction to him.

A man in his late forties sat at the desk in front of a bank of monitors. He looked up as they entered the security room. Gable made the introductions. "This is Brian Cookson. Right now his primary duty, along with three other security guards, is keeping unauthorized people off the island. Once the resort is opened, he will be head of security. Brian, this is Alexandra Caldwell. She's the researcher I mentioned to you. She'll be staying on the island for a few days."

Brian rose to his feet and extended his hand. "Miss Caldwell, it's nice to meet you. Anything I can do to help, just let me know."

"Thank you, Brian." The moment she accepted his handshake, a shiver of fear swept through her

Déjà Vu

body. This was a dangerous man, a very dangerous man. She attempted to quell her anxieties. Did Gable know how dangerous Brian Cookson was? Or had Gable hired him *because* of it? It presented yet another piece of what was rapidly becoming a confusing puzzle in the form of her host, Gable Talbot—an enigma decidedly turning more interesting than the thirty-year-old disappearance she had been hired to research.

Another loud clap of thunder underscored the tenuous hold she had on her composure. She managed to maintain her outer calm, but her insides refused to settle down. Why had her psychic abilities picked this time and this place to present her with the strange images? They had to have something to do with Gable Talbot, Skull Island, or the Hollingsworth disappearance. Or perhaps all three? Did it reinforce her notion that Gable Talbot might be part of the Hollingsworth family? But what specifically were the images trying to tell her? She had no more of an answer now than she did when the vision first popped into her mind.

Gable's voice broke into her thoughts. "Dolly will be preparing lunch shortly. She can serve you in the kitchen eating area. I have business to attend to so you'll be on your own for the rest of the day. Dinner will be served at six-thirty. We'll be eating in the dining room tonight since there are so many of us."

"Thank you for the tour. I'll unpack and start on my work. Obviously I won't be able to go outside today because of the rain, but in the meantime there's lots I can do in my room with the material I brought."

She turned toward the security guard. "It was nice meeting you." The look in his eyes told her more than she wanted to know. Yes, he was definitely someone to be wary of, someone to keep an eye on. But someone who posed a physical threat to her?

19

She didn't know.

****

Gable and Lexi left the security office, each headed in a different direction. As soon as they were gone, Brian walked across the room and shut the door. Ignoring the telephone in the office, he reached for his personal cell phone and made a call.

"It's Brian. She's here. Talbot just introduced her, then left her on her own for the rest of the day and returned to his meetings. It's raining hard right now, so she'll probably stay in the house. The others are supposed to leave day after tomorrow, assuming they get all their business done. He keeps his office locked when he's not using it. I checked the lock and it's much more sophisticated than a normal door lock. There's definitely something in there he doesn't want anyone else to see. It's going to be difficult to search his office without it being obvious that someone broke in."

Brian listened for a moment, then responded. "All but two of the windows in that room are sealed and the two that aren't only open a couple of inches, just enough to let in some fresh air. How do you want me to proceed?"

****

Lexi stared out the bedroom window at the non-stop downpour. After unpacking, she had set up her laptop computer and established a work area at the corner table where she could look out the windows at the ocean view...barely visible today.

A restlessness gripped her and refused to let go. Something was very wrong, or more accurately a lot of somethings were very wrong. The island...Gable Talbot...the security guard. As much as she wanted to blame her suspicions on an overactive imagination combined with the thunder and lightning, she knew that wasn't the answer.

The mental image continued to bother her. The

mud slide, being trapped in the muck, the skull, and the skeletons. Somehow she had to figure out what her psychic abilities were trying to tell her. If only she had control of them, knew how to use them. For years she tried to deny they existed, but had finally come to grips with the knowledge that neither the visions nor her concerns about what they meant were going to go away on their own. Maybe if she had accepted them when they started during her teen years, she would be more comfortable with them now. Possibly even able to control the visions and accurately interpret them.

She allowed a sigh of resignation. She couldn't turn back the clock. She was stuck with the here and now. And the here and now held a mystery she didn't understand and psychic images she couldn't explain. Were they a dire warning of some kind? A portent of danger? And if so, danger for whom? And from what?

She tried to shove her concerns aside and concentrate on her job. According to Gable, Dolly was preparing lunch for everyone. Getting acquainted with Dolly would be her first objective. As someone who had lived on the island a long time, she had probably made several observations and might be a good source of information...or at the very least some interesting gossip. Lexi left her room and headed for the main part of the house. Pausing at the kitchen door, she took a few moments to observe the short, plump woman at work before introducing herself.

Dolly appeared to be about sixty or so which would have made her in her late twenties when she and her husband first came to the island to work for the Hollingsworth family. Had they worked for Winthrop's father or had Winthrop hired them? She seemed pleasant enough as she scurried around the kitchen. Was the title of caretaker just another way of saying cook and housekeeper? And her husband, Hank...what duties did he perform? Maintenance man and gardener? Was it a lonely existence being the only people living full time on an island? Or were they the only ones living on Skull Island full time?

Of course, it wasn't as if they were truly that isolated. Skull Island was only a half hour boat ride from the Washington state mainland. The island had satellite television, computer internet, and all the other modern conveniences. Had they existed prior to the time when Gable purchased the island or were they part of his upgrades, installed when he built his private residence?

Lexi entered the kitchen. "Dolly?"

The older woman turned around. "You're Alexandra Caldwell?" Dolly smiled as she wiped her hands on her apron. "Mr. Talbot said you'd be arriving today to stay with us for a while. I imagine you're hungry. I'm just putting the finishing touches on lunch for Mr. Talbot and his business associates. You just sit yourself down at the table and I'll have something for you as soon as I deliver this tray to the office." She indicated the coffee maker on the counter. "The coffee is fresh. Help yourself."

Lexi returned Dolly's smile. "Thank you. Whatever you're cooking sure smells good." Another loud crack of thunder sent a tremor of anxiety up her spine. A low rumble followed, setting her nerves on edge. She poured herself a mug of hot coffee while wishing for something a little stronger to help soothe her nerves.

Dolly picked up the tray of luncheon plates and carried it toward the door as she called over her shoulder. "I'll be right back."

"That looks heavy. Can I give you a hand with it?"

"No thanks, dear. I'm strong. I can manage just fine."

Déjà Vu

Lexi sipped her coffee as she watched the rain splashing into the puddles on the large flagstone terrace. She opened the door and stepped out onto the covered wooden deck that extended the length of the house next to the terrace. The deck furniture had been covered and stacked up next to the wall indicating the end of summer.

Another boom of thunder ripped through the air sending a startled Lexi hurrying back to the safety of the kitchen. She tried to calm her anxiety by thinking about something else. Her thoughts gravitated toward Gable Talbot—his handsome features, mesmerizing presence, and dazzling smile.

She glanced out the window again. Hopefully the rain would not be one of those Pacific storms that lasted for days. Not only did it prevent her from exploring the island, she didn't feel comfortable using her computer with all the lightning. That pretty much confined her work to going over all the information she had previously printed out from the internet. There were also the old newspaper articles she had copied at the library. *This might be a good time for me to interview Hank and Dolly about the night of the party...the night three people disappeared from the island without a trace.*

The cool breeze grabbed her attention along with the sound of someone stomping heavy boots against the floor. She glanced toward the utility room and through the opened door into the garage where she saw a gaunt man of medium height in his sixties shrugging out of a bright yellow rain slicker. He hung the wet jacket on a hook, then sat on a bench and pulled off his muddy boots before entering the utility room.

"Dolly...has that—" he stopped in mid sentence when he looked up and saw Lexi. His gaze darted around the kitchen, then returned to her. A bit of a scowl wrinkled across his forehead.

"You'd be Miz Caldwell?"

"Yes." Lexi hurried toward the utility room with her hand outstretched. "I'm Lexi Caldwell. You must be Hank. I'm pleased to meet you. Dolly should be right back. She's delivering lunch to Gable's office."

He ignored her hand and her smile. "They still havin' them meetings? Thought they'd be done by now. How long does it take to say the golf course goes here and the swimmin' pool there?"

Lexi dropped her hand to her side, a little taken aback by his gruff manner. Hank and Dolly seemed to be a very mismatched couple, an unlikely pair. Dolly radiated good cheer as she bustled about the kitchen while chatting amiably. Hank, on the other hand, exuded a taciturn manner and acted more the part of the stereotypical crusty New Englander.

"Oh, Hank..." Dolly's voice entered the kitchen moments before she did. "I see you've met Miss Caldwell. The two of you sit yourselves down at the table and I'll set out some lunch." She turned her attention to her husband. "You must be chilled to the bone. I have some thick, hot beef stew and crusty French bread. It should taste good on a cold, rainy day like this. Something to stick to your ribs."

Dolly filled three bowls with stew and set them on the table. She glanced out the window. "It sure looks like we might be in for a long, cold winter." She returned her attention to Lexi. "This island is in a kind of sheltered location which protects it against the full brunt of the storms moving in from the Pacific. The winters are relatively mild compared to some of the other places in this area."

Lexi finished her lunch in silence as Dolly prattled on good-naturedly about any number of everyday topics. After everyone had finished eating, Dolly cleared the dishes. "If you'll excuse me, Miss Caldwell, I'll collect the dirty dishes from Mr. Talbot's office."

Déjà Vu

As soon as Dolly was out of sight, Lexi turned her attention to Hank. She offered a pleasant smile, one she hoped would put him at ease. "Mr. Talbot tells me you and Dolly have been the caretakers on the island for over thirty years."

"Yep, I reckon so. Somethin' like that."

"I guess that makes you a permanent fixture here…kind of like the Victorian mansion house."

He took a long drink of water from his glass before responding to her comment. "Yep."

A ripple of irritation told Lexi she would probably be better off trying to talk to the kitchen walls. They certainly couldn't be less responsive than Hank. She decided to give it one more try. "You must have seen a lot of changes on the island over that period of time. How many different employers have you had since you started working on Skull Island?"

"Couldn't rightly say." Hank stood up and headed toward the utility room door. "Gotta get back to work."

"I guess I'll see you later."

Hank didn't respond to her words. She watched as he went to the garage and pulled on his boots, shrugged into his rain slicker, and disappeared from view. She closed the door from the utility room to the garage. Was this his normal behavior or was he purposely being difficult and rude? Perhaps she would have better luck with Dolly, who was much more outgoing than her husband.

Dolly returned, carrying a tray of dirty dishes. She set them on the counter next to the sink, then looked around. "Did Hank leave?"

"Yes, just a minute or two ago. He said he had to get back to work."

"I'll swear…that man." Dolly allowed a sigh of resignation followed by a soft chuckle. "He works much too hard. I can't get him to slow down. Even on a day like this he's out there in the rain. One of these days he's going to catch pneumonia. I try to get him to take a rest after lunch, but he won't do it. He thinks he's still thirty-years-old rather than sixty-four."

"My father was like that. He never could just sit back and relax. He always had to be doing something. If there wasn't any work that needed to be done, he'd create some sort of a work project."

"That's certainly a good description of Hank." Dolly rinsed the lunch dishes, put them in the dishwasher, then wiped off the counter tops.

Lexi carefully formed her questions in her mind before asking them. "Gable tells me you and Hank have been the caretakers here for over thirty years."

"Oh, my...yes. Nearly thirty-four years. I never would have believed that I'd be living on an island for that long when we first came here. But it's been a good life."

"It struck me that being the only ones living on an island..." she paused for a moment as she cocked her head and shot a questioning look toward Dolly, "there have been times when it's been only you and Hank living here, right? That must have been a little lonely."

Dolly's expression became pensive as she wrinkled her brow into a thoughtful expression. "Oh...those times come and go. The last several years have been much quieter than the early ones with not nearly as many people coming and going as used to, but with Mr. Talbot's plans for the resort...well, I guess it will be real busy in the future."

"You were originally hired by the Hollingsworth family when they owned the island? Those must have been some exciting times if what I've read is correct. All the parties and things. I hear that it almost rivaled Hearst Castle in the lavishness of the parties and the notoriety of the house guests."

"Oh, my, Miss Caldwell. You're talking a time long before me and Hank was around. Charles Hollingsworth hired us three years before he died and Winthrop inherited everything. It was Richard Hollingsworth, Winthrop's granddaddy, who built the Victorian mansion, hosted all them parties, and had the house guests here all the time. That was in the 1920s and also the 1930s during the Depression. Those people are all long gone."

"Winthrop is an unusual name. I thought it might have been a family name, but you said his father was named Charles and his grandfather was Richard?"

"It's a family name, all right. It was his mother's maiden name. Charles Hollingsworth not only had family money, he married into money. The Winthrop family was wealthy in their own right."

"Wow…that must have made for quite an empire. And Winthrop Hollingsworth inherited all of that at the age of thirty-five?"

"Dolly!"

The sharp tone of voice grabbed Lexi's attention. She turned and saw Hank standing at the utility room door. A slight scowl and look of abject disapproval covered his face.

Dolly hurried toward the utility room. "Hank…I didn't hear you come in. Do you need something?"

"I need to talk to you," he shot a quick glance toward Lexi, "in private."

Lexi nervously cleared her throat. "Well, I need to get to work. Thank you for lunch, Dolly. It was delicious." She gave one last look in Hank's direction, then left the kitchen headed toward the glassed in walkway leading to the back section of the house.

****

As soon as Lexi was out of sight, Hank turned

his full attention to Dolly. He kept his voice low so no one else could hear him. "What do you think you're doin', woman? *He* ain't gonna like you givin' her all that information."

"Don't be stupid." Dolly fixed Hank with a stern expression. "I'm not telling her anything she can't find out for herself. If I'd been as rude as you she would of been suspicious and maybe started digging into something she'd normally ignore. The woman isn't a dummy, otherwise she wouldn't be doing the kind of work she does."

****

Lexi glanced at her watch, a little after five o'clock. She had been so engrossed in going over all the material she had brought with her that she had not been aware of the time. Over four hours had passed since she left the kitchen. She rose from the large comfortable chair, stretching her arms above her head as she walked over to the window. The rain had continued non-stop all afternoon and didn't show any signs of letting up.

The forecast called for the storm to move on before morning. Hopefully daylight would bring sunny weather so she could get outside and explore. She wanted to see for herself that the small cove on the far side of the island was the only place where someone could beach a boat and come ashore other than the dock by the mansion house. And if that was so, it also meant that was the only way off the island thirty years ago. She wanted to absorb the feel of the area, to put herself into the time and place when Winthrop and Evelyn Hollingsworth disappeared. That would require inspecting the inside of the mansion first hand rather than using photographs as reference.

She also wanted to spend some time with Dolly when Hank wasn't around. Perhaps Hank's reticence was his normal manner, but it seemed to

Déjà Vu

her as if he was purposely refusing to provide her with any information no matter how basic her questions were. It should have been obvious to him that she could easily obtain the answers elsewhere.

She took a deep breath and slowly exhaled as she turned her mind to other matters. Picking up all her work papers, she returned them to the appropriate folders. When she originally copied the many newspaper articles, she had made several pages of notes to go along with some information she had printed from the internet. She had spent the afternoon going over those notes. The material had been very helpful and opened up several areas of investigation that hadn't occurred to her when she first started her research. The entire history of the island after it had been acquired by Richard Hollingsworth fascinated her, particularly the time during the Prohibition period.

As she told Gable, she didn't know how J.D. Prescott planned to use her research information, but the activities that took place on Skull Island during Prohibition would be a terrific basis for a novel. Using Richard Hollingsworth as a real life model for a fictional character, much as Orson Welles was rumored to have done with William Randolph Hearst for his film *Citizen Kane*, could produce a best seller. Of course, that would certainly be quite a departure from Prescott's established style. She allowed a soft chuckle. Unless, as Gable had said, Prescott had the partially decomposed, gruesome looking bodies of the missing Winthrop and Evelyn rise from the ocean to terrorize everyone.

And again the image of the mud slide invaded her mind...the skull and the two skeletons. And again the image included her being trapped by the mud. A cold shudder swept through her body followed by an uncomfortable ripple of apprehension. *Could the two skeletons be Winthrop and Evelyn?*

Could they be terrorizing me because I'm delving into their disappearance? She shook away the disturbing thought. If they had been murdered, then why would their spirits object to someone trying to find out why and how? There had to be another answer and she needed to find it.

She turned her attention to dinner. Gable said they would be eating in the formal dining room with the three men she had met in his office. She took stock of the way she was dressed. Jeans and a sweater were not appropriate. She stared at the clothes hanging in the closet and finally selected a silk blouse with matching slacks. She freshened her makeup, dressed, then crossed over to the main section of the house.

"Lexi...join us, please." Gable's voice called to her from the den. "We're having a before-dinner drink. What can I fix for you?"

She entered the den, smiled and nodded her acknowledgement of the other three men, then walked over to the bar where Gable was mixing drinks. "Maybe a glass of white wine. Chardonnay?"

"Coming right up." He grabbed the chilled bottle from the wine cabinet, uncorked it and poured her a glass.

"I hope I'm not interfering with your business."

Fred Turnbull smiled at her, a smile bordering on a leer. "Not at all, young lady. I'd much rather look at you than these scruffy fellows."

She felt the heat of embarrassment flush across her cheeks. "Thank you."

"Besides, we've finished with everything on our to-do list for today and tomorrow we'll wind up our discussions and finalize a few items. I'm ready to return to my office and start work on the rest of the architectural drawings."

"Yep," Stuart Brooks spoke up, "I can tell you exactly where each hole on the golf course is going to

Déjà Vu

be, what type of rough along with the size of sand and water traps, and how each of the greens will break. When Gable sets a schedule, you can be assured everything and everyone adheres to it."

Walter Denning's laugh filled the room. "I hope I can keep my construction guys on schedule with the same success."

"So...tell me, Miss Caldwell," Fred Turnbull crossed the room to where Lexi stood at the bar, "how is your research coming along? Have you dug up any interesting new information? Uncovered any buried scandals of years past? Other than the obvious one from thirty years ago, of course."

"Please, call me Lexi." She extended a friendly smile, choosing to ignore the way the architect looked her up and down with a gleam in his eyes that projected only one obvious thought. "I've found a great deal of interesting information about the history of the island from the time Richard Hollingsworth purchased it in 1919—information that was new to me, but not anything that would shed light on the old police case or could be truly referred to as scandalous."

"Ah, yes...King Richard of the Hollingsworth dynasty who started with nothing more than the golden spoon in his mouth courtesy of his father's dealings in the Alaska gold rush."

Lexi cocked her head and shot a questioning look at Fred. "You seem to know quite a bit about the history of the Hollingsworth family." She forced a smile she didn't really feel. "Perhaps I should be interviewing you."

Fred ogled her. "It would be my pleasure to have you interview me, young lady. Or anything else you'd like to do."

Walter's laugh again filled the room. "Tell us, Fred...what would your wife think about that?"

Fred's laugh joined his. "I'm sure she wouldn't

like it, so let's don't tell her." He turned his attention back to Lexi. "I don't really know that much about the family history, just what I picked up while tracking down the original architectural drawings for the mansion. Richard's father...that would have been Winthrop's great grandfather...left his wife and infant son in Chicago and headed for Juneau, Alaska, when gold was discovered there in 1880. He managed to accumulate a decent amount of money and sent for his family. But he ended up carving out a very profitable niche for himself in Seattle by selling provisions to the prospectors and heavy equipment to the mine owners with the subsequent gold strikes in the 1890s in the Klondike region and then in Nome. He also became heavily involved in the lumber industry which brought him another fortune."

Fred lifted his glass toward Lexi in the form of a toast and gave her a quick wink. "Now you can say you interviewed me."

"That's very interesting. I hadn't anticipated going that far back in the Hollingsworth family. My plan was to only go as far back as Winthrop's birth, but I'm glad you shared that information with me. It gives me a better overview."

"Mr. Talbot—" Brian Cookson's voice interrupted as he entered the den. He glanced around the room before continuing. "There's something on one of the security monitors you need to see."

"Excuse me." Without further comment to his guests, Gable left with Brian close behind him.

The two men hurried to the security room. Brian pointed to one of four monitors, each displaying the picture of a different closed circuit surveillance camera. "It's difficult to make out much detail because of the rain, but it appears that someone is trying to beach a small boat in the cove. I sent Ralph

Déjà Vu

to check it out."

Gable stared at the somewhat blurry image on the monitor. Even though the cameras were state of the art and transmitted not only a sharp picture but also a thermal image back to monitors in the security office, there was only so much they could do to compensate for bad weather. He continued to watch what appeared to be a thermal image of a person in a small boat very close to the beach. The rough water buffeted him around as the boat neared the location where he could jump out, pull it up on the beach, and secure it.

A couple of minutes later a thermal image of another man appeared on the monitor indicating Ralph had arrived on the scene. The security guard quickly descended on the intruder and a moment later the two men were in a struggle. Gable's jaw tightened into a hard line. He didn't need to see the intruder's face. He knew exactly who it was.

Chapter Three

Ralph strong-armed the struggling man in his early thirties into the garage area of the house where Gable and Brian waited. "Look who I got here, Mr. Talbot. I guess *deporting* him to the mainland a couple of days ago didn't make much of an impression."

Gable stared at the tabloid reporter. "I sure hope your paper has a twenty-four hour hot line to a local attorney and bail bondsman because you're going to need it. Last time I took you back to the mainland and told you not to step foot on my private property again. This time I'm going to call the sheriff's office and press charges against you for trespassing."

Tom Jackson took a defiant stance as he squared off against Gable. "You can't intimidate the press. I have every right to pursue a news story and I have the First Amendment to back me up."

"The *press*?" Gable's six-foot-two stature towered over the reporter's five-ten height as he stepped in close and glared at the intruder. He made no attempt to hide the full weight of his contempt for the tabloid paper that employed Tom Jackson or for the reporter himself. "You don't really think the courts will uphold the notion that the scurrilous rag you write for is a legitimate newspaper conveying real news to the public in a timely manner, do you? And unless the government has recently rewritten the First Amendment, it does not give you the right to trespass on private property."

Jackson didn't back down from Gable's

Déjà Vu

aggressive action. "There's a story here. Thirty years ago a big name publisher and his wife disappeared while on this very island. So did one of their employees. It's an unsolved murder case. That's news."

"There hasn't been any evidence to say that a murder ever occurred. Maybe they bought another island somewhere and declared it a sovereign nation."

"Yeah?" The reporter managed a sarcastic sneer. "Well then that would be news, too."

"Yes it would—but *not* here on Skull Island!" Gable turned toward Brian Cookson. "Take our guest to the security area and call the sheriff's office. I'll definitely be pressing charges. If they can pick him up tonight, that would be great. If not, then find some place to put him until morning."

"You can't hold me here against my will. That's illegal!"

Gable allowed a wry grin. "Nonsense, Mr. Jackson. If the sheriff can't pick you up tonight, we're merely looking out for your safety until morning. It's far too dangerous out there on the ocean in that little boat of yours and I have no intention of endangering the life of any of my employees in attempting to get you back to the mainland."

He stared at Tom for a moment, then directed his comments to Brian. "See if you can dry him off. I don't want him dripping water through the house."

Gable's next instructions were directed to Ralph. "I hate to send you back out in the storm, but since you're already wet…"

A knowing grin turned the corners of Ralph's lips. "I know…since I'm already wet why don't I go back to his boat and see what he brought with him and make sure the boat is secured for the night. I'm on my way." With that, Ralph pulled the hood of his bright yellow rain slicker over his head and went back out into the storm.

Brian grabbed Tom Jackson's arm and ushered him toward the utility room. Gable surveyed the now empty garage with the large puddle of water on the floor where Ralph and Tom had stood. All the other newspapers—the *legitimate* ones—had played up the story about the mysterious disappearance of Winthrop and Evelyn Hollingsworth with only a minor mention of the disappearance of the employee. It was the tabloid paper Tom wrote for that had brought up Jack Stinson and repeated the gossip about the alleged affair between Jack and Evelyn.

And now this unethical tabloid reporter had again tried to sneak onto Skull Island—his private domain—in an attempt to dig up some dirt, disrupt his life, and interfere with his personal agenda. Gable clenched his jaw in anger. He hadn't anticipated the press jumping on things the way they did. If only he had set up the series of events differently, he could have had better control of the process. Well, it was too late for that now. He couldn't undo what had already been done. He would have to make the best of what had transpired and try to implement some damage control.

And tops on his *to-do* list was getting the very real distraction of Alexandra Caldwell off his island and out of his life. He would turn Tom Jackson over to the sheriff's department in the morning if the deputies hadn't been able to take the reporter into custody before then. His business associates would be leaving soon. Then he would deal with Lexi and her research. He renewed his determination and tried to shove his concerns aside. But he couldn't remove the pull of the physical attraction he felt toward her.

He wasn't sure exactly why, but when he gave her the tour of the house he had left out any mention of his master bedroom suite in its own wing with his personal outdoor deck and hot tub secreted behind a privacy wall separating it from the swimming pool and courtyard. But a quick flash of lusty desire told him why he had decided not to mention his bedroom.

He didn't have time to entertain lascivious thoughts about this woman...this beautiful woman who had knocked him for a loop when he first laid eyes on her. This woman who was nothing like what he had anticipated. Somehow in the back of his mind he had equated researcher with a stereotyped image of the spinster librarian, prim and proper with pinched features and her graying hair pulled back in a bun. Yes, indeed...Alexandra Caldwell was quite a surprise and definitely tempting.

Way too tempting.

Gable slowly shook his head to clear it of the unwanted thoughts as he walked to the utility room door. He came to an abrupt halt when he looked up and saw Lexi standing in the doorway. A quick jolt of anxiety hit him. How long had she been there? Had she witnessed the entire incident with the reporter? Was it something she intended to report to J.D. Prescott as part of her research? Things were definitely getting out of hand and needed to be reined in.

He forced a calm to his voice. "Is there something I can help you with?"

"Uh...no. I was on my way to the kitchen to see if I could help Dolly with the dinner when I heard voices." She looked around the empty garage, a slight frown wrinkling across her brow. "Is everything okay?"

"Everything is fine here." He reached the utility room door in four long strides, coming to a halt just inches from where she stood while flashing his most engaging smile. "Whatever Dolly is fixing for dinner sure smells good." It took all the restraint he could muster to keep from touching her. The fragrance of Lexi's perfume wafted across his senses. *And you smell really good, too. I can think of several things I'd like to...*

He shook away the totally inappropriate thoughts. For almost twenty-five years—since the age of fifteen—one thing had been uppermost for him, one item at the top of his list of things to do. He couldn't allow a very desirable woman to deter him from his goal. "I'll escort you to the dining room."

"Thank you." His smile may have said one thing, but she could tell from his eyes that it also hid something. He obviously had no intention of telling her anything about what had happened. The image exploded in her mind again. Mud sliding down the embankment, coming toward her, a skull, a skeleton, then a second skeleton. The same disturbing image over and over again, each time more baffling than the time before. Several times in less than a day. With repetition it had become slightly less frightening than the first time it happened, but it remained very unsettling.

A bright streak of lightning lit up the sky, followed immediately by a loud crack of thunder. A cold shiver darted up her spine and her heart beat jumped. Her body physically jerked to attention, causing her to bump against Gable. A moment later his arms were around her with his soft words calming her trepidation.

"Are you all right?" His voice carried his genuine concern.

"Yes...the, uh...the noise just startled me. I'm fine." She felt so safe, so secure in the comfort of his embrace. It only lasted a few seconds before he turned loose of her, but it was long enough to tell her she wanted more of this sexy man. First the psychic image and then the thunderstorm. And finally the tantalizing sensation of Gable's arms holding her.

Déjà Vu

Too many things all at once. She needed some quiet time to try and sort it all out. Perhaps after dinner...

Gable escorted Lexi to the dining room where the others were seated. The time passed amiably with casual conversation and a good meal. She took notes on the portion of the conversation relating to the resort plans, but even that was more general than specific. After dinner everyone returned to the den where Gable poured after-dinner drinks. Walter Denning and Stuart Brooks took their drinks to the game room where they knocked the balls around the pool table, leaving Lexi alone with Gable and Fred Turnbull.

Lexi took the initiative with the conversation, addressing her comments to both men. She had to keep the conversation focused on business, otherwise her thoughts would gravitate toward Gable Talbot, toward the strong attraction that grabbed her senses the moment she first came in contact with him. "I found your dinner discussion of the resort plans very interesting. Do you mind if I ask a few questions just to clarify a couple of points?"

Fred leaned close to her. "You can ask me anything you want, lovely lady."

"Thank you." Something about the architect left her uneasy. He openly flirted, but normally that wouldn't bother her. This, however, felt more like being sized up by a lecherous old man looking for a tasty treat. She leaned back in an attempt to put some distance between herself and Fred without appearing rude.

"I was wondering about the renovations you plan for the Victorian mansion. As I understand it, Richard Hollingsworth originally had the mansion built shortly after he purchased Skull Island." She paused as if a thought had just struck her. "Was there any type of a residence here prior to that?"

A bit of a frown wrinkled Fred's brow. "Well,

that seems to be more of a history question than anything to do with the resort plans."

She offered an apologetic smile. "You're right. It was something that just popped into my head. I thought you might know. It's not important. With regard to the mansion, do you plan to enlarge or add on to the original structure or simply remodel what's there?"

"Well, to accommodate what Gable wants, the plans call for remodel only. He wants to preserve as much of the integrity of the original mansion as possible. There will be several buildings constructed to provide the other services the resort will offer. The final result will be akin to a small country village that blends in with the natural environment rather than one large, crowded compound. The island is large enough to allow various areas to be spread out rather than grouped into one unsightly clump."

Fred gave a quick glance in Gable's direction. "All in all a very ambitious project, but it will be quite a stunning endeavor if it comes off as planned."

She immediately picked up on the use of the word *if*. Gable's expression gave no hint of his thoughts. Maybe the resort concept wasn't as much of a sure thing as she thought or as Gable Talbot had led everyone to believe.

"I would love to have a guided tour of the mansion, if that's possible." She cocked her head and raised a questioning eyebrow as she looked at Gable.

Fred rose to his feet. "I'd be honored to escort you through the mansion personally." He set his glass on the bar and held out his hand. "And there's no time like the present. Shall we—"

"Whoa!" Gable's amused chuckle interrupted Fred, but his eyes said that *amused* described neither his mood nor attitude. "It's still raining pretty hard. I don't think it's necessary to get wet for

Déjà Vu

something that can be done at another time and there isn't any reason to track mud inside unnecessarily."

"Well, then…" Fred winked at Lexi, his alcohol consumption beginning to show as indicated by his slightly slurred speech. "I guess I'll have to find another way to get you alone, my dear."

She responded with a nervous laugh as she tried to put a teasing, light-hearted spin on the strange turn the conversation had taken, at the same time distancing herself from what was becoming an uncomfortable situation. "As Mr. Denning said earlier, what would your wife say about that?"

"She definitely wouldn't like it." Fred sat on the bar stool and retrieved his glass, his expression saying he had heard her unspoken message.

Lexi shot a quick glance toward Gable, noting his unsuccessful attempt to suppress a grin as he raised his glass toward her. A subtle nod of his head and the twinkle in his eyes indicated his appreciation of her ability to handle the moment without creating a scene. A little wave of relief settled over her, alleviating her concern that she might have offended her host with her comments to one of his guests.

Brian entered the den, drawing her attention toward the door. He motioned for Gable to come with him. Gable excused himself, but gave one last unmistakable warning look at Fred before leaving the room.

"Sorry to disturb you again, Mr. Talbot. I've talked to the sheriff's office and they said they would send someone to pick up Tom Jackson in an hour. They didn't like the idea of sending out a couple of their deputies in a boat in this storm for a non-emergency, but when I mentioned Jackson's threat about being held against his will, they decided it would be better for everyone concerned if they took him into custody right away. The deputies will have the paper work for you to sign to press charges for trespassing."

Gable allowed a little sigh of relief. "Good. I wasn't looking forward to him making a public scene out of this. Take him down to the dock shed and wait for the sheriff's boat. Apprise them of the small boat Jackson beached on the far side of the island so they can notify the boat rental people to come and get it tomorrow."

He paused as he turned a thought over in his mind. "Don't mention anything about Ralph bringing the contents of the boat back here. If Jackson screams about his belongings, tell him he can retrieve them from the rental people after they pick up the boat. Call me on my cell phone when the deputies arrive and I'll go down to the dock and sign the paperwork."

"Sure thing, Mr. Talbot." Brian left to carry out his instructions.

Gable returned to the den to find that Walter and Stuart had rejoined the group. "Well, that was a short game."

Walter raised his hand as if wanting to be recognized. "My fault. No matter how hard I tried, I couldn't get any of those little balls to go into the pockets." He grinned at Stuart. "Lucky for me we weren't playing for money."

Stuart's reply said it all. "Next time we will be." The sly grin spread across his face. "Did I ever tell you that I worked my way through college by hustling suckers at pool?"

Gable unobtrusively removed Fred's glass from the bar and replaced it with a cup of black coffee. When he looked up, he saw that Lexi had spotted what he thought was an unnoticed action.

****

Ralph handed Gable a plastic bag. "I secured the

Déjà Vu

boat on the beach so it won't wash away or be damaged. This is what I found in it." He took off his rain slicker and shook away the water before hanging it on a hook on the garage wall, then took off his muddy outer boots. The security guard shook his head. "A little boat like that...it's a wonder he actually made it here in this storm. The jerk probably doesn't know how lucky he is. By all rights he should be at the bottom of the ocean."

Gable allowed a soft chuckle. "I'm sure the deputies who braved the churning waters to pick him up will let him know."

"Is that all you need tonight, Mr. Talbot?"

"Yes, thanks."

Ralph headed for the security room. Gable took the plastic bag and went to his office. Everyone else had retired to their respective bedrooms almost an hour ago. Dolly had finished in the kitchen and she and Hank had gone to their cottage. Gable was, at last, alone. It had been a long and exhausting day complicated by the arrival of Lexi Caldwell and the intrusion of Tom Jackson. Now he finally had some time to himself, time to revamp his personal agenda that seemed on the brink of deteriorating.

He turned on his computer and accessed a program he had written, entered his password to gain access to his files, then entered a second password that protected one very special file. If there was one thing Gable Talbot knew and knew well, it was how to protect his computer information. After all, he had started an internet company from scratch and sold it five years ago for one billion dollars. Several internet companies had sold for more money since then, but at the time it was an impressive amount. That certainly didn't put him anywhere near the Forbes list of the richest people in the world, but a billion dollars was a very tidy sum—money that allowed him to pursue the one

43

thing that had been an obsession for many years. And now the end was close enough that he could almost taste it. Most of the players were in position, ready to be manipulated along his pre-determined path.

So why was he being assaulted with sudden doubts? A foolish question. He knew the answer. Lexi Caldwell and her research. She represented an unknown factor in the middle of his carefully orchestrated drama. But was she truly a problem or just a minor inconvenience that he could circumvent? He wished he knew the answer to that. He also wished he knew why he couldn't get her off his mind and permanently out of his thoughts. And most of those thoughts about her were far removed from his carefully planned agenda. They were very personal, some of them even erotic in nature.

The way she looked, the way she sounded. It touched him on a very primal level. And that brief moment when he had steadied her after a loud crack of thunder caused her to jump...well, he could still smell the fragrance of her perfume and feel the texture of her skin as he held her. If he hadn't managed to turn loose of her when he did, he didn't know what he would have ended up doing.

But he sure knew what he wanted to do.

He shook his head as he forced his thoughts back to the work at hand. He had too much to do and had spent too much time working out the details of his plan to be detoured from his goal by the presence of a desirable woman...a *very* desirable woman. There was too much at stake. He turned his attention to the information showing on the computer screen. *Who knows. When all of this is over maybe I'll actually build that luxury resort. The more I see of the plans, the more I like the idea.*

****

Lexi poured herself another cup of coffee as she

stared out the window at the fog cloaking the island in a gray shroud. The rain storm had moved on during the night, but she hadn't been prepared for the fog that greeted her when she looked out her bedroom window that morning. Her mind drifted to last night and the subtle way Gable had handled Fred's drink.

It hadn't been Gable who poured Fred a drink. He had gotten it himself. If Fred had a drinking problem, why would Gable have hired him to do a project of this magnitude? Then Fred's words about *if it comes off as planned* jumped into her mind.

Was it possible that the entire luxury resort plan was a sham? That would explain why Gable said he was having second thoughts about having given her permission to do her research there. Maybe he was afraid she would find out that the project didn't really exist. Did he have outside investors who were putting their money into...into nothing? Then another thought struck her. If it was a sham, then why would he have agreed to her being there in the first place? What was he up to? Yes, indeed. Her host was becoming more interesting than her research assignment. The memory of his arms around her for that brief moment filtered through her consciousness and set her pulse to racing.

Yes...much more interesting than her research assignment.

"Do you want anything else before I clear the breakfast dishes from the dining room, Miss Caldwell?"

"No thank you, Dolly. I'll bring my coffee cup to the kitchen when I finish."

Her original plan had been to explore the island as soon as the rain stopped. But now she wasn't so sure. There wouldn't be much to see in the thick fog and even though the rain had stopped, it was still way too muddy. Gable would be tied up most of the day with his business associates who were scheduled to leave the next morning.

She took a sip of her coffee. Her spirit lifted a bit as she considered the other things she wanted to tackle such as inspecting the inside of the Victorian mansion to see where Winthrop and Evelyn Hollingsworth stayed while on the island. The fog wouldn't stop her from standing in the room where the party was held that night in order to get a feel for the atmosphere. Would Gable allow her to wander through the mansion alone or would he insist that someone be with her? She didn't want to abuse his hospitality or ruffle any feathers, but she preferred to look around on her own without someone hanging over her shoulder or intruding into her thoughts.

She carried her coffee cup into the kitchen, set it on the counter, then stepped out onto the terrace adjacent to the deck. The fog made it look cold, but the temperature was warmer than she had anticipated. When she saw Gable at lunch she could ask about touring the mansion. A noise from the kitchen caught her attention. She turned and saw Dolly standing at the door.

"Can I help you with something, Miss Caldwell?"

"I was wondering about the possibility of taking a walk even though I won't be able to see much." A hint of a sheepish grin tugged at the corners of her mouth. "I can use the exercise. After a day of traveling, then another day of being cooped up in the house because of the rain, I really need to do something active."

"Well...make sure you don't stray far from the immediate area of the house. I believe Mr. Talbot plans to eventually gravel the main walking paths, but for now they'll be terribly muddy. It...uh...might be better if you waited for a bit."

Déjà Vu

"Perhaps you're right. Thanks for the suggestion." Lexi glanced around the yard, at least as much of it as she could see through the fog. "This probably makes it difficult for your husband to get any work done, what with all the mud."

"Hank is working inside the carriage house behind the mansion. He uses it as a workshop."

The actuality and subsequent possibility hit Lexi with a surge of excitement akin to the light bulb of recognition being switched on. She cocked her head and leveled a questioning look at Dolly. "The mansion is unlocked? I'd love to see the interior."

A hint of concern covered Dolly's face. "I don't know. I think you'd best talk to Mr. Talbot about that. I know that architect fellow has been through it many times, but I don't know if Mr. Talbot wants people just wandering around in there."

Lexi offered a reassuring smile. "Of course. I'll talk to Gable about it at lunch." She headed toward her room in the back wing of the house. Was Dolly being helpful or purposely trying to put her off? She wasn't sure what to think. Every minute, things made less and less sense and her curiosity became more and more. Her curiosity about the island. Her curiosity about what really happened thirty years ago.

And especially her curiosity about Gable Talbot.

"Anything I can do for you, Miss Caldwell?"

Brian Cookson's voice startled her out of her thoughts. Where had he come from? She quickly glanced around, but didn't see anyone else. A lump of anxiety jittered in the pit of her stomach and an uneasy sensation settled over her. Something about him set her nerves on edge. If only she could figure out why.

"No, thank you. I was just going to my room to get some work done."

"Of course. If you need anything, just ask."

She watched as he went to the security office. His words and manner might have been polite, but his eyes were cold...and hard. A little shiver confirmed her thoughts about him as she returned to her room. Hopefully Gable would allow her to tour the inside of the mansion that afternoon. And in the meantime, now that the storm had moved on, she could safely get online without worries about the lightning. She turned on her computer. She had several hours before lunch and many things she wanted to check.

She accessed numerous members-only research websites, newspaper and university archives to gather additional information about the history of the Hollingsworth family and Skull Island. She dug deeper into both reliable news stories and tabloid type gossip about the disappearances. The main focus of all the news articles was the fact that Winthrop and Evelyn Hollingsworth had vanished without a trace. There were veiled mentions of the possibility of business rivalries being behind it and even one suggestion that gambling debts caused Winthrop and Evelyn to stage their own disappearances in order to escape the gambling czar's enforcers. That one didn't make much sense to her because Winthrop had more than enough money to pay any gambling debts, assuming he really had them. On a lesser note, and one followed more enthusiastically by the tabloid press, was the lurid speculation of an affair between Evelyn and Jack Stinson with Jack having turned to murder when he couldn't have the woman he loved.

Lexi tried to do research on Jack Stinson, but only came up with two items other than him working for Winthrop Hollingsworth. The first one mentioned that he had been divorced for three years with his ex-wife and son having moved to California.

Follow-up showed that they dropped from sight when Jack's name became linked to the disappearances. The second item dealt with Jack's twin brother, Robert Stinson, a world famous illusionist who performed under the name of Santorini The Great. He refused to give an interview to the press and would only say his brother was innocent of any wrong doing. Follow-up on Robert Stinson showed that he retired a couple of years ago and a few months later, there was a report of his death in an automobile accident in Spain. Both items led to a dead end.

Her thoughts returned to Gable Talbot, thoughts that were interrupted by someone knocking on her door. She quickly closed the file of notes she had been reviewing. A moment of anxiety assailed her senses when she opened the door and found herself face to face with Brian Cookson. She quickly glanced down the hallway hoping to see someone else in the area, but the guest wing appeared to be deserted.

Except for herself and the security guard.

She stood her ground, not giving him access to her room. "Is there something I can do for you, Brian?"

"Mr. Talbot wanted me to let you know lunch would be served in the main dining room in twenty minutes."

"Oh," she nervously shifted her weight from one foot to the other, "he isn't working through lunch as he did yesterday?"

"Apparently not, Miss Caldwell. Can I escort you to the dining room?"

"Thank you, but that won't be necessary. I have a couple of things to finish up first that should take just about twenty minutes, then I'll be there." She watched as Brian went back to the main portion of the house. She returned her attention to her work area and made a notation on a scrap of paper—*check out B.C.* After lunch she would see what kind of information she could find on Brian Cookson. It was probably only her imagination. After all, she had not observed him doing anything suspicious. And surely Gable would have run a background check before hiring him for a security position, especially if he was to be chief of security after the resort opened. But nothing she thought, no excuse she came up with, negated her feelings. The man set her nerves on edge. He radiated a sense of danger. It was only a feeling, but a very strong one that she couldn't explain.

Or perhaps a psychic warning of some sort?

And then there was that other feeling she couldn't explain, either. The one that said Gable Talbot was a man hiding a huge, dark secret.

Another knock at her door startled her out of her thoughts. A slight tremor of anxiety taunted her. Brian again?

Lexi called out toward the closed door. "One moment, please."

She quickly shut down her computer, then locked it and her papers inside her suitcase. It wouldn't stop anyone from going through her things, but it would require breaking the lock on her suitcase to do it. After taking a calming breath, she opened the door and found herself staring up at Gable's mesmerizing green eyes and handsomely chiseled features. The calming breath totally vanished. Her pulse raced and her mouth went dry. She tried, but couldn't force out any words.

Déjà Vu

Chapter Four

Gable's smooth voice sent a tingle of excitement through Lexi's body. "I wanted to make sure you were going to join us for lunch."

"Uh…" She desperately fought to regain her composure. "Yes." What was there about this man that set her heart pounding and knocked her senses sideways? She had been around handsome men often enough for it not to have an untoward impact on her ability to function. But suddenly she felt like a tongue-tied school girl rather than a mature woman in control of her life. "Brian said lunch was in twenty minutes, so I decided to finish up a couple of things before going to the dining room."

"Brian?"

"Yes…when he came to escort me to the dining room as you asked him to." She glimpsed a moment of hesitation flash across his features and just as quickly disappear, almost as if he wasn't sure he had heard her correctly. It lasted only an instant, but it left her a little unnerved.

"Are you ready?" He flashed an incredibly sexy smile. "I'll walk you over."

As with dinner the previous night, lunch consisted of Lexi, Gable, and his three business associates. From what Lexi could gather of the conversation, they had basically concluded their business discussions and would only be taking care of a couple of loose ends following lunch. The boat would pick up the three men that afternoon and transport them back to the mainland rather than in the morning as originally scheduled.

Following lunch, Dolly entered the dining room to collect the dishes. While Lexi still had Gable's attention, she voiced what had been on her mind. "Would it be okay with you if I took a tour of the mansion this afternoon? The rain has stopped, but it's still too foggy for me to do much exploring around the island and it would probably be a waste of time to try to take any pictures until I can actually see what I'm photographing. And, of course, there's all that mud. I feel a need to get out and do something rather than sitting at my computer." A hint of a sheepish grin tugged at the corners of her mouth. "I really do need to move around and get some exercise."

"You're certainly welcome to use the swimming pool. I find swimming to be a great exercise."

Was he purposely putting her off? Trying to switch her attention to something else? Or was it nothing more than a logical suggestion? She forced her thoughts into a more practical pattern. She had to curtail the way her imagination kept running wild. "Unfortunately, I didn't think to bring a swim suit. Since the resort hadn't been built yet, it never occurred to me that there would be a pool available, let alone an indoor one."

Then he allayed her concerns and at the same time made it clear that her suspicions were unfounded. "You can look around inside the mansion this afternoon if you'd like. Or if you can wait until tomorrow when I'm free, I'll be glad to show you around."

She offered what she hoped would be a neutral smile that did not carry even a hint of what she thought. "Would it be okay if I did both? Maybe take a cursory look this afternoon, snap some pictures, get my list of questions together, then you can give me an in depth tour tomorrow and answer my

Déjà Vu

questions?"

He captured a moment of eye contact with her as if trying to peer into her mind and know what she really thought. "No problem."

Gable turned toward Dolly as she placed the dirty dishes on a tray. "Would you tell Hank to let Lexi into the mansion so she can look around?"

"Certainly, Mr. Talbot." Lexi noticed the quick narrowing of Dolly's eyes, the only hint of any negative thought passing through the older woman's mind.

Fred Turnbull's voice cut into the conversation. "I have something here that will probably be helpful to the lovely lady." He smiled at Lexi as he took a sheet of paper from a file folder, his smile seeming to once again be more of a leer. "I made extra copies of my sketch of the floor plan in case we needed them. It seemed more practical for general discussion than to wrestle with those large blueprints." He handed the sketch to her.

"Thank you, Fred." Lexi glanced at the drawing. "This will be very helpful."

She returned to her room to gather her thoughts about the mansion and what she wanted to investigate. She took a few minutes to study Fred's detailed drawing, typical of an architect. The mansion was much larger than she realized with many more rooms than she had thought even after seeing it from the road. The first floor contained an entrance foyer, formal living room, two smaller parlors, a billiards room, formal dining room, kitchen with informal dining area, three bathrooms, and a very large ballroom that opened onto a terrace through four sets of French doors. There seemed to be some type of an enclosure connected to the ballroom that had an outside entrance, but Fred had not identified it. With the exception of the informal dining area off the kitchen, the entire first floor seemed to be for the purpose of entertaining guests whether personal or business related.

The second floor contained guest accommodations consisting of twelve bedrooms and six bathrooms split evenly on each side of a central hallway with every two bedrooms sharing one bathroom between them.

The third floor consisted of a combination business office and owner's private retreat. One end of the hallway held a small conference room and office along with a half bath. The rest of the floor had four bedrooms, each with a private bath, an informal common room including a television viewing area, a kitchenette, and eating space for the family's private use. The drawing indicated a dumb waiter going from the main kitchen on the first floor to the kitchenette on the third floor. Many of the rooms in the mansion had fireplaces, undoubtedly from the days prior to central heating.

Lexi grabbed a light weight jacket and shoved a mini audio recorder and her digital camera into her pockets. She wanted to be able to record her thoughts and any questions that occurred to her as she looked around. And being alone, she could take pictures of what she wanted without someone else wondering why she found that particular thing important.

After getting directions from Dolly of where to find Hank, she left the house and set out on the paved road that led to the dock, the same one Gable had used to drive her to his house when she arrived. She hadn't gone very far before the fog totally obscured Gable's house. She stopped walking, closed her eyes, and took in a deep breath. The air smelled of a brisk combination of rain, damp leaves, pine, and the ocean. She listened. Rather than the fog shrouding any sounds, it seemed to enhance them. She could hear fog horns, a couple of boats, the

Déjà Vu

waves hitting the rocks, and even seagulls. She also heard some type of pounding, most likely whatever Hank was doing.

Then the image exploded in her mind again. The mud sliding toward her, the out of focus face, the skull, and finally the skeletons—this time more vivid than any of the previous assaults on her senses. A cold shudder moved up her spine, followed by a lump in her throat and a churning in the pit of her stomach. She hugged her shoulders in an attempt to fend off the shivers, but not from the cold. Her insides trembled to the point where she felt as if she had no control over her own body. Even though she still didn't understand the message trying to get through to her, this time the vision truly frightened her on both a physical and emotional level.

This time it felt very real...and very personal.

She tried to shake off the uncomfortable feelings, but without much success. Then a new sensation hit her, an eerie awareness of someone watching her. Someone obscured by the fog. Someone laying in wait. Someone wanting to harm her? The possibility sent a hard jolt of fear racing through her veins. It played on her already tautly stretched nerves. A genuine sense of alarm welled inside her. She fought the desire to run blindly down the road. But toward what? And away from whom? One thing loomed abundantly clear...she needed to move on, to get away from this spot that radiated a feeling bordering on evil.

Lexi hurried down the road toward the mansion as she fought against the almost uncontrollable urge to continually glance over her shoulder. The panic built, layer upon layer. The danger close on her heels, almost as if it could reach out and grab her. Only the paved road under her feet offered any comfort or relief from the overwhelming sensation. The large Victorian mansion became visible through the fog, but would it provide a sanctuary? A safe haven?

She paused in front of the carriage house behind the mansion, taking a minute to catch her breath. The noise coming from inside told her Hank was at work. She furrowed her brow into a bit of a frown. If Hank was there, then it couldn't have been him watching her in the fog. Logic...she needed to put some logic to all of this, to somehow ground her fears. She tried to gather her determination. Surely the vision of the mud and skeletons triggered the eerie sensation of being followed. Her imagination had obviously run amuck. In truth, there wasn't anyone watching her. Sucking in a calming breath, she opened the door to the carriage house.

"Hello, Hank. I'm sorry to interrupt your work. Dolly told me I'd find you here. Gable has given his permission for me to look around inside the mansion. Would you unlock the door for me, then I'll get out of your way?"

"Dolly told me you'd be 'round this afternoon wantin' to snoop inside."

"Well," she allowed a nervous chuckle she hoped sounded casual rather than filled with the irritation his comment created. "I don't think *snoop* is appropriate. It's part of my job and Gable did say it would be okay."

"Ain't nothin' much to see." Hank reached in his pocket and withdrew a key ring, then left the carriage house at a swift pace headed toward the mansion. His abrupt departure left her scrambling to catch up with him.

"I'd love to sit down with you and Dolly when you have a few minutes and talk to you about what it has been like working here. The changes over the years with the different owners. The differences between working for Winthrop and working for his father." She cocked her head and raised a

Déjà Vu

questioning eyebrow. "Maybe even test your memory of what happened the night of the costume party when Winthrop and Evelyn disappeared?"

"Like we told the sheriff back then, me and Dolly don't know nothin' about it. We was busy workin' in the kitchen when the storm knocked out the power. We wasn't invited guests in the ballroom enjoyin' the party with the upper crust of society."

Hank glared at her, then unlocked the front door without making any further comment. Lexi watched as he returned to the carriage house, leaving her alone on the front porch of the old Victorian mansion.

The moment she entered the foyer, her previous anxieties disappeared. It felt as if she had stepped through a portal into another place and another time. She closed her eyes for a second as the sensations washed over her. She could visualize the days of conspicuous opulence that accompanied the Roaring Twenties. Prohibition with its bootleggers and homemade bathtub gin. Jazz. Flappers. Lavish parties. A magnificent tribute to the extravagances of the wealthy in times gone by. The power and influence of the celebrities, politicians, and captains of industry who had been guests in the mansion during the days when Winthrop's grandfather owned the island, before the stock market crash of 1929 brought the country to its knees, followed by the years of the Great Depression.

When the island had been inherited by Winthrop's father, Charles had kept the mansion preserved in its original style and decoration while modernizing plumbing, heating, and electrical. A year after Winthrop's disappearance, the estate had sold the island. Subsequent owners had also chosen to keep all but the top floor of the mansion in its original style while upgrading the kitchen and bathrooms.

And according to what Fred had told her, Gable intended to do the same even though the mansion would now be the main building of a luxury resort. The resort guest rooms in the mansion would maintain the style of the original rooms as would the lobby and other common rooms such as the restaurant, café, cocktail lounge, and gift shop.

Assuming Gable actually intended to build the resort.

And what about Gable himself? Just being around him made her pulse race, yet she couldn't ignore the mixed signals he seemed to be sending her way. One minute his attitude said he didn't want her on the island. Then he not only included her at dinner with his business associates, he showed up at the door of her room to make sure she joined them for lunch rather than eating in the kitchen with Dolly and Hank as she had done the day before. And even to the point of asking if he could escort her to the dining room.

Maybe her visions didn't make any sense yet, but one thing had become very clear. She found Gable Talbot as fascinating as he was mysterious. Perhaps doing research on her host should be a priority. Although she didn't have a rational explanation for it, she didn't believe his story about living off family money. But the fact remained that he seemed too young to have acquired enough money on his own to buy Skull Island and build a resort. Assuming the money actually belonged to him. Again, the thought popped into her mind. Could he be the key figure in an investment scam?

She pulled the recorder from her pocket and pushed the record button. "Check amount of money paid for Skull Island and the amount of the mortgage held by the lending agency." She turned off the recorder, thought for a moment, then clicked it on again. "Also any information available on Gable

Talbot." The mysterious Gable Talbot, as captivating as he was enigmatic.

And so very desirable.

After putting the recorder in her pocket, she took out the small digital camera and wandered around the ground floor. Everything she saw captured her interest—the furnishings, the accessories, the rooms themselves. Beautiful hardwood floors. Crown molding. She picked up several objects in the living room, inspected them, then put them back where she found them—any one of the period accessories probably worth a great deal of money. She immediately noted the lack of dust on the furniture. Did Dolly clean the mansion on a regular basis in addition to taking care of Gable's house? That was a lot of work for one woman and she wasn't that young anymore. Perhaps Gable did his own cooking, laundry, and daily picking up after himself. Or maybe Dolly had made a special point of cleaning the mansion due to the presence of Gable's business associates, especially with the architect and contractor being in and out of the mansion during the course of the meetings.

Lexi checked out the other rooms on the ground floor, then opened the double doors with the beveled glass inserts and took one step across the threshold into the ballroom. An unsettling wave crashed through her, carrying vibrations of deception, danger...and murder. This was the room where Evelyn and Winthrop were last seen. When she cautiously ventured farther inside the magnificent ballroom, the feeling disappeared as quickly as it had arrived.

She stood in awed silence as her gaze traveled around the large room and took in the exquisite and lavish surroundings including the crystal chandeliers. She finally managed one word. "Wow!"

The expression on her face totally mesmerized

Gable as he stood back from the double doors, watching her. As soon as he had dropped off his business associates at the dock where they boarded the boat for the mainland, he floored the accelerator of the electric cart and headed straight for the mansion. When he found the front door unlocked, he knew she would be inside.

Alexandra Caldwell had occupied far too many of his thoughts since her arrival. He had spent a long time on the intricate details of his plan. He didn't have time to devote to figuring out why he found her presence so alluring or what there was about her that made him want to pull her into his arms and kiss her long and hard. He watched her for a few seconds longer. And the more he observed of her, the more he wanted to know everything about her.

But caution rang loud and clear in his head. What did J.D. Prescott really want with the research about Skull Island and the resort plans? Or was it actually J.D. Prescott who wanted it? Exactly what role did Lexi play in all of this? Had her letter about researching for J.D. Prescott been honest or did she have some hidden scheme of her own? He only had her word for the fact that she had been hired by Prescott. *Damn. I hope she's not one of those investigative reporters looking to write a book about a thirty-year-old disappearance.* Now that his meetings were concluded and business associates gone, perhaps it would be prudent if he confirmed her identify.

All his carefully constructed plans could be in jeopardy. Yet he couldn't stop his thoughts about her from straying to the personal.

To the *very* personal.

"It certainly tells a tale of days gone by, doesn't it?"

Lexi physically jumped at the sound of his voice

and whirled around until she faced him. An audible sigh of relief escaped her throat. A smile spread across her face as she put her hand next to her pounding heart. "You scared the hell out of me!"

"I'm sorry." He walked across the room to where she stood. "I thought you heard me come in. I should have called to you from the front door."

"That's quite all right. I was so absorbed in the atmosphere of this room that I probably wouldn't have heard you." She glanced around the ballroom again. "This room fascinates me." Her gaze fell on an object for a second or two before moving on, her obvious appreciation growing with each new item she encountered. "The parties must have been the epitome of elegance and grace. How marvelous that all the owners through the years chose to leave the mansion in its original state, especially this room."

"Only this floor and the second floor with the guest bedrooms have been kept in their original style with the exceptions of the necessary upgrades to kitchen, bathrooms, and the electrical wiring. The third floor is contemporary. In fact, it's almost like a self-contained apartment. If this house was on the mainland and the third floor had a private entrance, it could be considered a rental unit separate from the rest of the house. With four bedrooms, it would accommodate an entire family. I haven't quite decided whether I'm going to break it up into individual rooms, suites, or keep it intact to rent to a large group such as family members vacationing together."

"Why didn't you take over the third floor as your personal vacation property rather than build a different house just across the small meadow?"

"Because I wanted the privacy and separation from the resort..." He reached out and touched her cheek, an involuntary gesture that he couldn't have stopped even if he wanted to. "And its employees and guests. The bulk of the resort buildings will be located in the opposite direction from the mansion than my house."

"Then why not...uh...why not on the other side of the island rather than so close to the mansion?"

Consciously he knew he needed to back off. Intellectually, he knew he didn't dare start something that might side track him from his all-important primary agenda. But he didn't seem to be able to stop himself from twining his fingers in her hair. He heard her quick intake of breath and saw a combination of confusion and what he hoped was desire dart through her eyes. The silky tendrils fluttered across his skin, accompanied by a tightening in his chest. His gaze dropped to her slightly parted lips, a mouth that beckoned to him. One that needed to be kissed thoroughly and often.

Gable's grasp on his will power had been tenuous at best. In an incendiary flash, the final traces of self-control totally deserted him. He brushed his lips against hers, not knowing what to expect from her in return. There was a moment's hesitation on her part, something more akin to surprise than uncertainty. Then he felt her soft touch on the back of his hand as it rested on her cheek. She didn't pull away from him. It was all the encouragement he needed.

He pulled Lexi into his embrace as he lowered his mouth to hers again. It started out as a gentle kiss, one having as much of a surprisingly emotional feel to it as it did a hard rush of physical desire. Her arms wound around his neck and her mouth responded. She tasted of sweetness and passion, an enticing combination. And he wanted more.

Much more.

But years of planning and preparing could not be set aside. He had initiated his carefully worked out scheme. There would be no turning back until he

Déjà Vu

had achieved his goal. Nothing...and no one...would deter him.

He threaded his fingers in her hair again. As much as he needed to get on with his own business, he was not ready to stop the delicious kiss. He came within a breath of exploring the recesses of her mouth with his tongue, of tasting the tantalizing essence of the woman who had continually intruded into his thoughts from the moment the boat delivered her to his island.

He held her tighter, caressing her shoulders and running his hand down her back. Knowing he needed to step away and put some physical distance between them pulled at him equally as strong as the knowledge that he couldn't relinquish his hold on her.

Lexi was the one to break off the kiss, but she did not step away. The spell she cast over him had not been broken. He quickly captured her mouth again, but held the kiss for only a couple of seconds before relinquishing his hold on her. Even though he took a step backward, he couldn't bring himself to eliminate all physical contact. He continued to clasp her hand, slowly lacing their fingers together.

He forced some words in a desperate attempt to bring the situation back to a neutral place, to where he had control of his desires. "How much of the mansion have you seen? Have you been upstairs yet?"

Her answer came out as a breathless whisper. "I've only been on the first floor."

"Then allow me to take you on a tour of the upper floors. If you have any questions, I'll be glad to answer them." He led her toward the massive curved staircase that went to the second floor landing then continued up to the third floor.

It was a smooth transition as if the kiss had never happened, except for the fact that he continued to hold her hand. They ascended the stairs and he took her through each of the guest rooms. Then they continued to the third floor.

She experienced an immediate sense of loss when he released her hand and stepped aside at the top of the staircase so she could go through the door to the third floor. It had taken her a moment to recover from the surprise when his mouth came in contact with hers, then she had willingly accepted his control. Everything about the kiss definitely exceeded her fantasies about him. Excitement had coursed through her body. The sensation fulfilled everything she had hoped it would and more.

A new thought clouded her mind. Where was this headed? She knew in an instant where she wanted their spontaneous encounter to lead. But there was nothing practical about that thought. She didn't know anything about Gable Talbot other than the fact that he made her pulse race and her heart pound. Finding out who he was topped her list and until she knew, she couldn't allow herself to become physically involved with him.

It took her a moment to get her bearings as she looked around. It was like leaving the 1920s and being transported to the here and now in the blink of an eye. All the furnishings and decoration were contemporary including the flat panel high definition television.

"This is certainly an interesting contrast..." Her words stilled in her throat as his gaze locked on hers in an intense moment of eye contact. It took all her self-control to keep from touching her fingers to her lips as the lingering excitement of his kiss rippled through her body.

She finally managed to force out some words, her voice not as firm as she would have liked. "Uh...did you make these changes or did you buy it this way? Was the mansion fully furnished including

Déjà Vu

this modern apartment?"

"I haven't done anything to the mansion since I purchased the island. To the best of my knowledge, all the furnishings are original from the time the mansion was built except for the third floor. The previous owner renovated this floor and his family used it as their vacation home while preserving the first and second floors in their original state. I do intend to install an elevator so guests won't need to deal with the staircase unless they want to."

A tremor of anxiety made its way through Lexi's body, replacing the sensual reflections of the kiss. She had just caught Gable in an absolute lie. She had recently been shopping for a new television and recognized the one in the common area of the third floor. That particular model of flat panel high definition television was first manufactured only two years ago and Gable had owned the island more than four years. It couldn't possibly have been purchased by the previous owner of Skull Island. Why the deception? What purpose would there be in him claiming to have not done any of the contemporary upgrades to the third floor? And for that matter, since he had his own house why would he have purchased a new television for the mansion at all? Had he used the third floor during the construction of his house? But again, why lie about something as insignificant as that? It made no sense to her. Yet it had just happened. One more piece to the puzzle.

They returned to the first floor where Lexi wanted to take one more look around the ballroom. "This is the last place Winthrop and Evelyn Hollingsworth were seen? Is there any information confirming where they were standing in this room? Over by the French doors that lead directly outside? In the middle of the room on the dance floor? Maybe close to the double doors at the ballroom's entrance?"

Caution ruled Gable's response. "There might be something in the sheriff's report from that night, something witnesses told the deputy, but I don't know anything about that. Apparently the storm knocked out the power. By the time candles were lit and flashlights were found, Winthrop and Evelyn were gone."

"But wouldn't the house have been on some type of generator system for power rather than the equivalent of power lines strung on poles from a substation as it is on the mainland? It seems unlikely that the storm could have knocked out the power under those circumstances."

"I really don't know. You'll need to check with the sheriff's department to see what's in their report from that night."

The smell of her perfume tickled his senses. The tightness pulled across his chest again. Conflicting needs controlled his actions—on one hand, his need to stop the direction of her questions and on the other hand, his need to once again sample the sweetness and passion he had experienced with their first kiss.

He knew he shouldn't, but he managed to shove his concerns aside as he pulled her into his arms again and took control of her mouth with a passion filled kiss that spoke volumes about the sensuality of the man. A moment later a flash of panic darted through Gable's consciousness. This time he broke off the kiss.

Alexandra Caldwell represented everything in his life that he had put on hold until after his plan played out to the conclusion. She was too dangerous to be around, a deterrent to his carefully worked out agenda. Yet he could not deny the way she made him feel or his desire to have her body entwined with his.

He brushed his lips against hers again, then quickly stepped away. Running his hand across the

Déjà Vu

back of his neck, he sucked in a calming breath. Not that it did any good. The only thing that could put a stop to his immediate pursuit of her was for him to turn his back and walk away from her tempting presence.

"If you don't have any questions you want answered right now, I need to get back to my office. I have work to do and some emails to send before the close of business today." He turned toward the front door of the mansion, then paused. "Please feel free to stay here as long as you'd like. Let Hank know when you've finished so he can lock the door."

Lexi stood motionless as she watched Gable walk away, closing the door behind him as he left the mansion. Again, she felt a sense of loss even though the heat of his kiss lingered on her lips. Neither of them had mentioned the first kiss the entire time he had shown her around the mansion, as if it never happened. It had helped to eliminate some of the awkwardness of the moment, but to continue to pretend that it didn't exist...well, it would be just as easy to try and swim back to the mainland.

She pulled in a deep breath, held it for several seconds, then slowly exhaled. It helped a little, but her insides still quivered from the excitement of his kiss. She sucked in another lungful of air, shook her head in an attempt to clear the unwanted thoughts, then headed for the front door.

After letting Hank know he could lock the mansion, she started back to her room. A moment of apprehension shivered through her as she approached the area where she had experienced the sensation of someone watching her. She hurried along the path, willing the uncomfortable memory to go away. A sudden thought invaded her mind. Why did Gable keep the mansion doors locked when there wasn't anyone on the island? Hank and Dolly both had access with a key, so who was Gable locking out? Granted...there were many items of value in the mansion, a reality separate from the lurid speculation of the disappearances, but that still didn't explain it. After all, he didn't keep his own house locked up tight.

Determination pushed her forward. Gable Talbot became her primary task for the rest of the afternoon. By dinner, she hoped to know enough about him to be able to make an accurate judgment as to why he felt the need to be so deceptive. Dinner...it would be just the two of them. Her mind wandered to what the night would bring, an uncomfortable direction for her thoughts to travel.

But an equally tantalizing one.

Lexi checked the lock on her suitcase. Satisfied that no one had tampered with it, she took out her laptop computer and quickly connected with the internet. For the next two hours she concentrated her efforts on finding out everything she could about Gable's background—his family, where he came from, where his money came from, and how much he had paid for Skull Island. The public records listing the purchase would provide her with some viable information. She remained deeply absorbed in her work as the remainder of the afternoon slipped away.

Nearly six o'clock. Lexi stood and stretched the kinks out of her back. Dinner would be served at six-thirty. Shaking her head in dismay, she locked her computer inside her suitcase again. Her research into the life and times of Gable Talbot proved as mystifying as the man himself. According to what she found, he purchased Skull Island four and a half years ago, paying ten million dollars without taking out any type of property loan or mortgage.

A ten million dollar cash sale? The island had originally been put on the market at nine million

Déjà Vu

dollars with speculation that the owners would be receptive to a lower offer. He had paid one million dollars above the asking price in order to shut out any other potential bidders and expedite the process so he could get immediate possession. And that wasn't the most bothersome thing she discovered. The information she turned up proved every bit as baffling as the Hollingsworth disappearances.

No record of Gable Talbot existed prior to five years ago when the object of her research suddenly materialized from nowhere with his fortune in hand. He was only a child at the time of the disappearances thirty years ago, not old enough to have had any involvement. So, why did he want ownership of Skull Island so badly that he willingly paid one million dollars more than the owners were asking and apparently in cash as soon as the island had become available?

Who was this man hiding behind the name of Gable Talbot?

Chapter Five

A million questions swirled through Lexi's mind during dinner, questions she was afraid to ask for fear of what the answers might be. Gable, on the other hand, seemed to be more relaxed and open than he had since her arrival. Could it be because he had finished his business meetings and the other men had left the island? Had the emails he sent resulted in some good news?

And still no mention of the incident in the mansion as if the kisses had never happened. Kisses that literally curled her toes and took her breath away. Kisses from the sexiest man she had ever encountered.

They carried their after-dinner drinks to the den where Gable built a fire. She sat on the carpet with her back against the sofa, facing the fireplace. Even though Hank and Dolly were still in the kitchen and the security personnel on duty, it felt as if the two of them were all alone. Two people sharing the beauties of an otherwise deserted island. The fog started to lift allowing patches of starry night sky to show through. He turned off all the lights, leaving only the illumination from the flames highlighting his handsome features.

She had never known a more desirable man...or a more mysterious one. Who was he? Why would a false identity be important to him? A dangerous criminal living off the ill-gotten gains from a series of spectacular bank robberies? A jewel thief enjoying the proceeds from millions of dollars of stolen

Déjà Vu

diamonds? An embezzler who siphoned a fortune from a huge international conglomerate? Is that what J.D. Prescott suspected? Was that the information he really wanted when he hired her to do research? One thing she believed to be true...whatever Gable was hiding fit into the riddle surrounding her.

The visions...the premonition of danger. Somehow it all fit together. A cold chill moved up her spine in defiance of the warmth from the fireplace. Could she possibly be in danger if she discovered the truth? But in danger from whom? She closed her eyes and leaned her head back, resting it against the sofa cushion. The disturbing possibilities swirled around in her mind. And most disturbing were the visions of the mud sliding toward her, entrapping her in the ooze, followed by the appearance of the two skeletons.

Lexi heard him move, then settle on the floor next to her. He smelled good, a combination of aftershave and a masculinity that grabbed her senses and wouldn't let go. In spite of her apprehension about the secrets he kept, she couldn't shake the intense pull of his sexual magnetism...nor did she want to.

"How is your research coming along? Are you finding what J.D. Prescott wants?"

The sound of his voice, a sensual whisper in her ear, sent little shivers of delight dancing across her skin. "Well, it's not going as smoothly as I had hoped. I've come across a few surprising bits of information, but I haven't been able to put it into context...yet." Perhaps because she had run into a brick wall when she shifted her research to her prime concern and current major focus—discovering the truth about Gable Talbot.

"Maybe I can help. What seems to be puzzling you?"

She gave him a sly sideways glance. Maybe he could help? He certainly could. All he needed to do was confess his true identity and tell her why he chose to hide behind a façade. "Now isn't that curious. I thought you told me you didn't know anything more about the disappearances than what you read in the newspapers." Another little tremor of excitement assailed her senses as he ran his fingers across her cheek and down the side of her neck.

"Well...you're right." He forced what he hoped sounded like a casual yet embarrassed chuckle. "I guess I really can't be too much help in that department after all." *Damn...I walked right into that one. What is there about this woman that has my thinking so muddled?* He knew the answer before he had even fully formulated the question in his mind. Smart, beautiful, sexy, able to handle herself in an awkward situation with grace and style. It still pleased him when he thought of the way she had put Fred Turnbull in his place when he tried to hit on her...tactful, ladylike, but leaving no doubt about what she meant. She was everything a man could want.

And a terrific kisser, too.

His gaze ran across her features and came to rest on her lips...her very kissable lips. Once again it proved a temptation too strong to resist. The kiss started simple and innocent, but quickly escalated to match the passion churning inside him. The long time obsession that had resulted in his personal agenda and grand scheme occupied all his time, especially for the last few years starting with the creation of his new identity. It left little room for a personal life. But even at that, his relationships had always been discreet. Quality mattered more to him than quantity. He had never felt a need to see how many different women he could get into his bed and how often.

In spite of the demands on his time, Alexandra Caldwell was one woman he could not ignore. No way could he view her as a casual encounter, a temporary diversion...a one night stand. He also knew mere kisses weren't going to be enough.

He flicked the tip of his tongue across her lower lip, then invaded the dark recesses of her mouth. Exploring, tasting, teasing. Each breath he drew turned more ragged than the one before. Each thought strayed farther from the reality of what he should be doing. His fingers threaded through the soft strands of her hair, the texture more like silk than anything else.

Her arms circled around his neck and shoulders as she fully responded to his advances. He liked that. No silly little games or pretenses. No manipulation or attempt to control the situation. It all seemed to happen so naturally, to flow from the desires of two people obviously attracted to each other. At least on his part the attraction could not be denied regardless of how much he wanted to put it aside...to save it for a time when he would be free to explore the possibilities without encumbrances. But for now...

Gable wrapped his arms around Lexi, bringing her with him as he leaned back on the floor. He settled her body on top of his, caressing and stroking her shoulders and back. All the while his mouth teased, his tongue tasted, his lips nibbled. His hand slid down her back and came to rest on her rear end. Everything about her excited his senses and aroused his libido. In fact, arousal was about to be one of his problems. If he wasn't careful he'd have a full erection and, with her body on top of his, no way to hide it from her.

Shifting his weight, he maneuvered her off his body and onto the floor. Their tongues twined in a type of ritual akin to a precursor of making love. Her taste filled his mouth with a need for more. The tantalizing fragrance of her perfume teased his senses. He had never been so intensely or so quickly attracted to any woman as he was to Lexi. He tried to tell himself that he couldn't afford the distraction, not at a time when his plan required all his energy and attention. Then the concern vanished in a heated flash of incendiary passion. He slipped his hand beneath her shirt and ran it up her back, savoring the creamy texture of her skin. His last viable thought told him to put a stop to his seduction while he still could...before it went beyond his control.

Lexi took the decision out of his hands before he had time to make the choice. With a little whimper of regret, she broke off the kiss and pulled back from him.

"Gable...this isn't...we shouldn't..."

"I know..." He folded her in his embrace, tenderly holding her close, but nothing more. His voice dropped to a whisper, part regret and part frustration. "I know."

****

Brian Cookson walked silently down the hall toward Gable's office. A quick glance into the den had told him Gable would be busy for a while and would most likely be adjourning to his bedroom very soon. Lexi Caldwell was a tasty looking morsel. He wouldn't mind having a go at her himself. But for right now, he had business to tend to. He had been studying the special door lock on Gable's office and had finally figured out how to circumvent it. He had two objectives—the contents of Gable's safe and the files in his computer. The door lock had been a true challenge, but he suspected it was nothing compared to what he would find with the safe and the computer.

Wherever Gable came from and whatever his

true identity, one thing had become evident. He knew all about security. Even the infrared wireless surveillance cameras monitoring the cove and the dock had been his doing right down to the choice of manufacturer and model of the equipment and its placement at the site.

Per the clandestine instructions issued to Brian when he first arrived on the island, he had done as thorough a search as possible of Gable's belongings with particular attention to the office. That foray had resulted in the discovery of the sliding panel hiding the location of the safe. Unfortunately, it had been the last time he had access to the office due to the fancy new lock Gable had installed on the office door.

But now his careful study of the new lock had proved successful. After gaining entrance, he went directly to the sliding panel all the while listening for anything that sounded like someone approaching the office door. Definitely a risky move, but the way things had been going it might be his only chance. He had to choose a time when he was the only security guard in the house, the only one on duty. No way he could hang around late at night after someone else relieved him in the security office. Hank and Dolly were not a concern, or so he had been informed. But caution still remained the order of the day.

As soon as he got a close look at the safe, he knew he wouldn't be opening it...at least not that night. Another of Gable's unique security features. That left only the computer. He turned it on, but didn't hold out much hope for success. As expected, the entire system was password protected. He attempted to hack past it and gain access only to run into an even more sophisticated password protected security wall, a program he had never seen before and didn't have the vaguest idea how to manipulate.

Gable Talbot definitely knew his way around computers, too.

Brian quickly removed all signs that he had been in the room and hurried back to the security office. He slowly shook his head as he mumbled his thoughts out loud while reaching for his cell phone. "Damn! He's not going to like this."

****

Lexi slowly opened her eyes. The bright, early morning sun filtered in around the edges of the drapes. She stretched her legs, wiggled her toes, then threw back the covers and climbed out of bed. Her lips still tingled from Gable's kisses and the memory of his touch continued to warm her skin. The evening had been a strange one...part mutual seduction and part tender moments of quiet togetherness. Sexual tension had filled the air and that wasn't all.

Regardless of whether she wanted it to be so or not, she couldn't deny that her emotions had become involved. Gable Talbot—a virtual stranger, a man she had just met, a man of mystery hiding dark secrets behind a false identity. Yet a man who had managed to invade more than just her thoughts. A man who touched her emotions as surely as the sun rose in the east.

What would this new day bring? Would it be like the first time...neither of them mentioning it as if the passion hadn't erupted between them? Knowing they could have just as easily ended up in bed, but hadn't? She wasn't ready to face Gable that morning. The confusion continued to swirl around in her head as she showered and dressed. Instead of going to the kitchen for breakfast, she went to the small kitchenette area in the guest wing. She made some coffee and poured a glass of orange juice. The sunny morning provided the first nice weather since her arrival and she intended to explore the island.

Déjà Vu

The images exploded in her mind, sending her reeling backward a couple of steps. *Get out!* She squeezed her eyes tightly shut while pressing her hands against her temples and shaking her head from side to side. *Get the hell out of my head!* But the images refused to leave. The out of focus face, only this time it had more definition to it before morphing into the skull, enough so that it had recognizable features but not any that looked familiar to her—a face she did not know. A wall of mud sliding toward her, holding her captive. One skeleton, then a second one. Her heart pounded. Her breath came in quick gasps to the point where she almost felt light-headed. The intensity...the urgency...the frightening reality. Images much more vivid than the previous ones. Panic tried to grab her, to fill her consciousness. To warn her. But warn her of what? The vision kept repeating, always the same images, but each time a little more clearly defined. Slow deep breaths...one after another...control her breathing. Stave off the mounting panic. The images finally faded away.

Somehow Gable fit into the puzzle, a key piece that could go toward explaining what seemed to be unexplainable. She felt it. She *knew* it as surely as she knew her own name. It was her initial meeting with Gable—the moment they shook hands while standing on the dock—that had triggered the first vision. If only she could figure out where and how that incident fit into the overall scheme of things.

Forcing the thoughts from her mind, she slipped into her jacket, then shoved her camera and mini-recorder into her pockets. She set out on her exploration, starting along the same route she had taken the day before when she went to the old mansion. She took a few minutes to snap some pictures of Gable's house and then the mansion with its incredible Victorian architecture. The main road

77

led ahead toward the dock. A foot path branched off and turned inland, away from the edge of the cliff.

Her step quickened as she made her way along the path, although she wasn't sure exactly why she felt the need to hurry. After all, she wasn't going anywhere specific and she certainly didn't need to adhere to a time schedule. She looked around. This was the location where it happened yesterday. A brief moment of anxiety resurrected the uneasy sensation of being watched, the flash of panic that warned of danger. Then the memory of being enfolded in the security of Gable's arms shoved away the uncomfortable feeling. She pushed the reminiscence aside. No way could she allow the distraction of the sexiest and most handsome man she had ever encountered to keep her from her goal.

A man who made her insides quiver with desire.

Quiver with desire? She came to an abrupt halt. A tremor of anxiety jittered its way through her body. That thought had to be banished immediately before it took hold and became a reality, one she couldn't afford to entertain. At least not at the present time.

Lexi resumed her stroll. The foot path meandered across a small meadow, then passed through a wooded area. Sunlight glistened off the wet leaves. Mottled patterns of light and shadow covered the ground. She paused to take some more pictures of the beautiful scenery, then continued her walk. The path emerged from the woods along the edge of a shallow ravine on the other side of the mansion.

A moment of shock paralyzed her. The breath caught in her lungs. She fought to maintain her balance while the world crashed around her. Then the ground gave way beneath her feet. Panic grabbed every corner of her existence. A cold shiver started small and grew with each passing second.

She tumbled into the ravine, totally out of control both physically and emotionally.

Panic turned to utter terror. The blood pounded in her ears. Her heart beat hit her chest with the booming thud of a timpani drum. An ear piercing scream filled the air. It took a moment for her to realize the scream had come from her throat.

Her mind tried to assimilate everything as the surreal scene unfolded in front of her in a bizarre form of slow motion déjà vu. She looked up from the bottom of the ravine. The wall of mud cascading down the side filled her view. Mud sliding toward her, engulfing her feet and legs, trapping her like wet cement. Her legs refused to obey her mind's commands. She froze to the spot. The out of focus face that had earlier plagued her visions sharpened into a face with distinctive and clearly defined features for a fleeting second before morphing into a skull.

Then the bones appeared.

It seemed so real. It *felt* so real, but was it still a vision solely in her mind? A cold, clammy sensation crept across her skin. A frightening chill invaded every conscious fiber of her body. A skeleton tumbled from the side of the embankment, falling toward her. A moment later a second skeleton emerged from the gaping hole in the side of the ravine. Another scream ripped from her lungs and throat, filling the air with her terror.

Her heart pounded so hard it literally hurt. She attempted to scramble to her feet, but the more she struggled the tighter the mud held her. Then the most horrifying moment of all. The skeleton landed on top of her. Not a vision. Not a dream. Not her imagination. Not a hallucination.

A very real skeleton.

Lexi flailed wildly in an attempt to escape the terrifying nightmare that engulfed her. Only it wasn't a nightmare. Her vision had become a frightening reality.

Mud. Bones. The more she struggled, the more enmeshed she became. *Focus...focus...stop struggling...think...think...calm down.* She fought the panic rapidly stealing her logic and common sense. Almost as an involuntary action, she forced her breathing into a slower rhythm, taking deep breaths and holding them for a couple of seconds before exhaling. A partial sense of control finally settled over her. She called for help. But was there anyone within earshot? Anyone who could hear her?

Then her newfound control dissolved into another jolt of panic when her gaze fell on Brian Cookson. She frantically scanned the surrounding area, as much of it as she could see from the bottom on the ravine, but didn't see anyone else. Totally at the physical mercy of whoever found her, the last person she wanted to see stood at the top of the ravine looking down at her.

"You all right, Miss Caldwell?"

An unnatural calm surrounded his words, one that definitely rattled her nerves even more than they already were. He stood there, not making any attempt to help her. His voice contained an unusual monotone that left her even more on edge than she had been. It took all her resolve to keep even a modicum of rational control. *Hell no! Any damn fool could see that I'm most certainly not all right!* She did her best to bring a semblance of control to her words, one she definitely did not feel. "I...I don't know...I think so. I'll know better when I get out of this mud. I can't pull myself free."

Then the most wonderful sound reached her ears, a sound that shot a welcomed wave of relief through her consciousness.

"Hurry, Hank. It's Miss Caldwell. She's had an accident." Dolly appeared on the scene a moment after Lexi heard her voice.

An unmistakable shock spread across Dolly's face, then all the color drained away. Her features twisted into a mask displaying all the horror coursing through her veins. Her hand flew to her mouth, but not in time to stop the startled gasp from escaping her throat.

Then a moment of absolute clarity hit Lexi. Dolly's attention was not on her and her plight. It had become fixated on the skeletons.

"Dolly!" Hank's sharp voice brought his wife back to the here and now. "Go fetch Mr. Talbot."

Dolly stared at Hank without responding to his orders, her eyes wide with fear. A mask of confusion covered her face. She didn't make any effort to move as if she hadn't heard what he said.

Hank grabbed her arm. "Dolly! I told you to fetch Mr. Talbot. Right now, go!"

Dolly shook her head, as if to clear her thoughts. "Uh…yes, of course." She turned and hurried away.

Hank focused his attention on Lexi. "You be calm, Miz Caldwell. We'll have you outta there straight away."

He glanced at Brian. "You gonna stand there like some dumb ass or you gonna give me a hand here?"

Brian paused for a second as if unsure about what to do. Then the two men jumped down into the ravine. Using their hands, they scooped mud away from her body. Without any tools and mud continuing to ooze from the gaping hole, it took about fifteen minutes to clear her legs and the lower part of her body. Hank grabbed her under the arms to pull her clear.

"Lexi!" Gable charged toward the ravine at full run. Dolly followed close behind driving one of the electric carts. He immediately took charge.

"We'll get you out of there, Lexi. Stay calm.

Everything's going to be okay." A moment later Gable stood in the ravine, up to his ankles in squishy mud. He picked her up in his arms, gently lifted her out, and set her on the surrounding ground. He quickly scrambled out of the ravine. After helping her to her feet, he escorted her to the cart and wrapped her in a warm blanket. "Will you be all right here for a few minutes before going back to the house?"

"Yes. I'm fine now." She attempted to lighten the moment. "I think my heart has started to beat again, but I must look a mess."

He extended a relieved smile as he wiped some mud from her cheek. His voice teased. "You look lovely...in an interesting sort of way." Then his manner turned serious. "Are you sure you're okay? Nothing broken or sprained?"

"Nothing I'm aware of."

"You stay put. I'll be right back."

While Gable used his cell phone to call the Sheriff's Department and report the discovery of the skeletons, Lexi rummaged around in her jacket pockets looking for her camera. Hopefully it hadn't been damaged. Ignoring Gable's orders to remain in the cart, she ventured toward the ravine. A moment of apprehension caught her as she approached the edge, but she gathered her determination and continued.

She snapped several pictures of the skeletons including close-ups of the skull, pieces of clothing tangled with the bones, and some other items she didn't immediately recognize even though they seemed to belong with the skeletons. And while she was at it, she grabbed some candid shots of Gable, Brian, Hank, and Dolly...although she couldn't say why she felt compelled to do it.

Gable disconnected from his call to the sheriff's office. His attitude all business, his demeanor saying

Déjà Vu

he had control of the situation, he turned toward Brian. "Call me on my cell phone as soon as the deputies arrive. And don't touch anything here. I don't know what Lexi fell into. It could be some sort of centuries-old Native American burial site. There might be several more skeletons in this area. Whatever it is, we can't compromise the scene. If the crime lab determines that the bones are truly old and there isn't anything connected to illegal activity requiring the sheriff's attention, the anthropology department at the university would most likely be interested. And that will undoubtedly bring in the attention of the local Native American tribes. The one thing I want to do is keep this as quiet and low profile as possible. I don't want any more press coverage than we've already had..." An angry look crossed his face, "...especially from the tabloids."

Gable directed his attention to Hank. "Check the rest of the path along the ravine for any other unstable areas."

After giving Hank his instructions, he focused on Lexi. He didn't like what he saw. He had left her safely ensconced in the cart, but there she stood at the edge of the ravine. "I thought I told you to wait in the cart."

Raising a questioning eyebrow, she cocked her head to one side. "*Told* me? As in issuing an order as if I was one of your employees?"

Even though she sounded tough and in control, he could see the confusion and anxiety in the depth of her eyes, an emotional chaos that touched him on all levels. "No, not as if you were my employee. Rather as someone who is concerned about you. Not only have you had a jarring physical accident, falling into a ravine and being half buried in mud, there's also the psychological impact. The fear of being buried alive. The horrific reality of the skeletons..."

A hint of an embarrassed smile tugged at the

corners of her mouth. "If you're trying to soothe my rattled nerves, you need to rethink your method. Talk of being buried alive doesn't quite get it."

He ignored her attempt to put him off. "What you've been through is enough to unnerve the strongest of people."

He grabbed her hand, led her back to the cart, and drove to the house. Every few seconds he shot her a sideways glance. More than her safety swirled through his mind. When Dolly had located him in his backyard and told him about the skeletons, it all exploded in his mind so clearly. His comments about an ancient burial ground were nothing more than window dressing. He didn't want to be the one who stated a connection to the disappearances. Didn't want to suggest that the case had been solved...well, not really solved. But finding the skeletons proved the disappearances were not voluntary. Two people had been buried and the notion that they buried themselves was ludicrous. The door to the past he had been searching for had finally been opened and he intended to take full advantage of it.

But before anything else, he needed to make sure Lexi was really okay and not just telling him what she thought he wanted to hear.

"The first thing we need to do is get you out of those muddy clothes and into a nice hot shower."

"Oh? *We* need to do that, do *we*?" Was he purposely making suggestive comments to distract her? To keep her from dwelling on the magnitude of the accident? Her literal brush with death? A quick shiver told her just how close she had come to serious injury...or worse.

"Stop being difficult. You know perfectly well what I mean. Although..."

A teasing twinkle in his eyes and a sexy grin did nothing to calm the sudden rush of desire that flooded through her. A steamy shower, wet skin

Déjà Vu

against wet skin, more hot kisses that took her breath away. Making love...

Lexi forced her thoughts to the pictures she had taken, especially the ones at the ravine. She definitely wanted out of her muddy clothes and into a nice shower and clean clothes. But what she really wanted was to download the pictures into her computer to confirm that her camera had been functional and the memory card protected.

Gable drove the electric cart into the garage and plugged it in to recharge. They each kicked off their muddy shoes, then he escorted her into the house. He insisted on walking her all the way to her bedroom. Once inside, he closed the door, then pulled her into his arms.

"Are you sure you're all right?"

"Yes. Just a little banged up, that's all. Nothing broken or apparently even sprained. But I'm sure I'll be sore in the morning."

"I want you to get in a nice hot shower right now. Give me your muddy clothes and I'll have Dolly launder them for you."

"There's no reason to inconvenience Dolly with this. With all the mud on my clothes, it's not like they can be thrown in with some laundry she's doing anyway. I'll get in the shower with these clothes and rinse them that way before taking them off. Then after I take a shower, I can run them through the washer and dryer myself."

"Well...tonight, before you go to bed, I'm going to insist that you soak in the hot tub. It will help ease tomorrow's aching muscles."

She flashed a warm smile. "Now that's a suggestion I can agree with."

As soon as Gable left, Lexi rushed to put her plan into play. She pulled off her muddy clothes and threw them into the shower, then washed the mud from her hands, arms, face, and neck. After cleaning the exterior of her camera, she removed the memory card and made sure it was clean. Fifteen minutes later, she had showered and washed her hair, hung her wet clothes over the bath tub, and dressed in clean clothes. She glanced at the clock. According to what Gable had said, it would still be another half hour before the sheriff's deputies arrived to investigate. Enough time to download her pictures...if there were any pictures available to download.

To her relief, the memory card had not been damaged. After transferring the pictures from the card to her computer hard drive, she did a cursory check of what she had captured but did not study them. She would save that for later. She wanted to be present when the deputies arrived on the scene.

Déjà Vu

Chapter Six

Lexi stood on the dock watching Gable as he took the line thrown from the sheriff's boat. A moment later, three men and a woman disembarked, all wearing sheriff's department jackets with appropriate credentials hanging around their necks.

Gable shook hands with the man obviously in charge. "Bud, it's good to see you. Wish it was under better circumstances." He indicated Lexi. "This is Lexi...Alexandra Caldwell, the unfortunate person who happened to be walking next to the ravine when the mudslide happened. Lexi, this is Deputy Sheriff Bud Lansing."

"Miss Caldwell, nice to meet you." They shook hands. "We'll need a statement from you, exactly what happened and in the order that it happened."

"Of course, deputy. I've been going over it in my mind and think I've sorted out all the pieces."

Bud introduced the rest of his team consisting of another deputy and two crime scene investigators, each carrying a work kit. "Now, how far are we from the scene?"

"Less than half a mile using the existing road and path. I brought the large electric cart with me. Should be adequate to transport your team and equipment. Are you ready?"

Gable drove everyone to the site of the mudslide. Only Brian Cookson had remained at the ravine, as instructed. He greeted Gable. "Hank and Dolly went back to their cottage. Hank was covered in mud." He glanced down at his own muddy uniform.

Bud took out his notepad and pen. "You were the first one on the scene, Brian?"

"Yes, I heard Miss Caldwell calling for help and rushed over here to see what was wrong and found her in the ravine, stuck in the mud. Hank and Dolly arrived a moment later. Hank sent Dolly to the house to find Mr. Talbot, then we started digging the mud away from Miss Caldwell. We had just freed her legs when Mr. Talbot arrived."

"Okay. Go ahead and get cleaned up. We can finish this later."

"Thanks, Bud. I'll hurry back as soon as I can. I'll have Ralph stay in the security monitoring room to cover the start of my shift."

Lexi watched as Brian walked away. No way would her screams have carried back to Gable's house, let alone to anyone inside the house. So, what had Brian been doing in the area of the ravine? He was in uniform, but apparently a couple of hours away from the start of his shift. What had he been doing that wouldn't allow him time to change before going to work? Hank and Dolly's cottage was very close. Could Brian have been on his way either to or from there? But why? What would have been so important that he needed the privacy of their cottage rather than talking to them at the house at lunch time?

She warily approached the edge of the ravine and looked down inside. One intact skeleton, the scattered bones of another, plus the skull. Pieces of clothing. She pulled her camera from her pocket.

The female crime scene investigator called out to Lexi. "I'm sorry, Ms. Caldwell. You can't take any pictures. Until we figure out exactly what we have here, this is considered a crime scene."

"Of course. I apologize. Is it okay if I take pictures of the area as long as I don't take pictures of the ravine?"

Déjà Vu

The woman glanced toward Bud Lansing who had been listening to their conversation. He gave a slight nod of his head and she returned her attention to Lexi. "That will be all right."

Lexi walked away from the ravine. Gable could probably procure copies of the official photographs which would be better pictures than what she could take. She needed to inform J.D. Prescott of what had happened. He would expect photos of the area. One of his concerns was knowing exactly where construction and landscaping would take place. Having the side of a ravine collapse and two skeletons fall out would most likely come under that heading. She took several pictures of the general area, noting in her mind where existing buildings were located in relation to the local scenery. But was there really any reason for her to send him copies of her photos showing the skeletons? As things stood right now, no one knew she had taken pictures before Gable drove her back to the house to clean up.

Hunger pangs rumbled in Lexi's stomach. Juice and coffee for breakfast, no lunch, and enough adrenaline pumped into her veins to keep her on edge for a week. Not exactly a well balanced diet.

"Well…I guess someone has to say it…"

Lexi looked up at the sound of Bud's voice in time to see Deputy Lansing level a serious look in Gable's direction.

"These bodies have probably been here for thirty years. It looks like we might have found the missing Winthrop and Evelyn Hollingsworth."

Gable stared at the bones in the bottom of the ravine. "After all these years…"

"We'll transport everything back to the lab, then start the procedure to officially identify them."

"Of course. Keep me apprised of what you find. I'm sure I'll be needing some kind of answers for the media when this gets out."

"Sure thing, Gable."

Lexi and Gable watched as the crime scene investigators went through the meticulous process of documenting the scene with photographs, collecting everything, tagging it and sealing it in containers. Brian returned and Deputy Lansing pulled him aside to finish taking his statement.

And all the while Lexi kept a cautious eye on Hank and Dolly. Hank remained his usual taciturn self, but Dolly still seemed very frightened, almost on the edge of emotional collapse. The discovery of skeletons would certainly be unnerving, but it wasn't Dolly who had been caught in the mud slide. So why would she be so obviously distraught? Strange. Very strange, indeed.

****

As soon as the team from the Sheriff's office left, Hank and Dolly returned to their cottage. A very frightened Dolly stared at her husband. "What are we going to do? This isn't at all what we'd been led to believe."

"Hush up, woman! Get yourself under control. Ain't much we can do but keep our mouths shut. Maybe them skeletons are part of some old Indian burial ground like Mr. Talbot said."

"You know that's not true. Weren't Indian trinkets with those bones. The bits of clothing were costumes like the party that night. You and I both know those bones belong to Jack Stinson and Evelyn Hollingsworth. When they discover that's not Winthrop Hollingsworth, you can be sure there's going to be a whole new round of questions for us. We need to find out what *he* wants us to say. This makes everything different. It's not what he told us. Jack and Evelyn didn't run off together."

"Yeah, we're gonna need some instructions all right."

"I'm scared, Hank. I think you should call him

now."

"You're right." He grabbed his cell phone and dialed an unlisted phone number. After four rings, the call was answered.

"This better be very important for you to call me."

Hank nervously cleared his throat. "Yes, sir. It is. All the rain...the storm...well, the side of a ravine gave way. That researcher lady, the one I told you about who's working for that writer...well, she got trapped in the mud...and..."

An irritated reply assaulted Hank's ears. "Get the hell to the point!"

"They found two skeletons." Only silence greeted Hank's statement. "You still there? What do you want us to do?"

"You don't know anything. You're as shocked as everyone else. As far as what happened thirty years ago, tell the same story you told then."

"But you told us Jack and Evelyn had run off together and you needed to go into hiding because you knew everyone would suspect you of foul play. And now there's them two skeletons...I mean...uh...what happened?"

"I'm as surprised by all of this as you are. Must be that Jack killed her then killed himself. A murder suicide rather than them running off together. Now you really need to keep me out of this. If anyone knew for sure I was still alive, they'd be hunting me down to try and blame me for this. You make sure you communicate with me on a daily basis from now on so I'll know exactly what's happening."

With that, Winthrop Hollingsworth disconnected from the call.

****

Following dinner Gable escorted Lexi to the den and poured them each an after-dinner drink. Lexi felt at a bit of a loss, uncertain about how to handle things. She wanted to get back to her room and study the photographs she had taken. Regardless of what Gable had said, she agreed with Deputy Lansing. The bones were the first step in solving the thirty-year-old disappearances. But were they really Evelyn and Winthrop Hollingsworth? As long as Jack Stinson remained part of the equation, nothing could be taken for granted until the lab officially identified the skeletons. And today's forensic science provided many more avenues of identification than the dental charts that would have been the only means of accomplishing it thirty years ago.

But she could not deny that she also wanted to spend time alone with Gable. And her reasons were two-fold. First was the undeniable attraction between them, apparently on his side as well as hers. She had never experienced such a strong attraction to a man before, one she definitely wanted to explore. Then there was the mystery of Gable Talbot himself and his true identity. She again toyed with the notion that he might be part of the Hollingsworth family, a possibility she intended to dig into and research until she had some answers.

However, for right now, she liked the idea of him taking care of her. The concern he demonstrated for her safety felt much more personal than someone simply making sure she hadn't been injured. The feeling settled over her like a warm security blanket.

Gable brushed his fingertips across her cheek while making eye contact. "Are you sure you're okay? No latent injuries making themselves known?"

"I wish you'd stop asking me that. I'm fine. The anticipated aches are setting in, but I'm sure they'll be gone in a couple of days." A moment of contemplation interrupted her words, a thought she didn't want to acknowledge even though her words escaped into the open. "Just in time for me to return home to finish my assignment for J.D. Prescott." She broke the eye contact and tried to shake away a truth she didn't want to deal with while attempting to lighten the mood. "Although I must admit my research has been far more fascinating than I thought it would be." And the most fascinating part of all…Gable Talbot.

"I'm afraid those aches will definitely cramp your style in the morning and they'll probably be accompanied by plenty of bruises, too. There isn't anything I can do about the bruises, but I have a viable treatment to help ward off those aches." He stood, took her hand, and pulled her from the chair. "Let's get into the hot tub."

He led her down a long hall and a minute later they stood at the double door entrance into a wing he had not originally included as part of the tour. "This is my private area, including my secluded deck and hot tub." It had all happened so naturally. He told himself he couldn't get involved with her, especially not when he was so close to putting his full plan into action. Besides, he didn't really know that much about her which in itself wasn't that big a deal, but with everything else going on it could be a crucial element. And the discovery of the skeletons had certainly accelerated the time table and put much more at risk. Yes, all things he knew for a fact.

And, right or wrong, knowledge he chose to ignore.

Something completely unexpected had happened to him when he heard about the mud slide. And then when he saw her, so frightened and so vulnerable, he couldn't put his growing emotional involvement aside as easily as he had previously been able to. Somehow he needed to work out all the angles so everything would fall into place. Another couple of days and the last element would be at the ready and he could make his second big announcement regarding his plans for Skull Island.

But for tonight...

"Uh...Gable...I didn't bring a swimsuit. It never occurred to me that you would have an indoor pool or a hot tub I could use." A chuckle, part amused and part nervous tension, escaped her throat. "Of course, it never occurred to me that I would end up at the bottom of a ravine covered in mud while being attacked by skeletons."

He opened the door so they could go inside, then shoved the door closed with his foot as he pulled her into his arms. "I'm sure we can find some sort of solution to this swimsuit problem."

Before she could respond to his purposely suggestive comment, he captured her mouth with a passion filled kiss that left no confusion about his intentions. And to his joy, she responded to his unasked question with a silent answer that said she wanted him as much as he wanted her. Their previous kisses had bordered on the hot and heavy, kisses that spoke of desire and passion. Tonight would be about physical desires with the logic of right or wrong relegated to tomorrow's concerns.

Gable reluctantly broke the kiss. Two warring factions tore at him. He wanted her more than he had ever wanted any other woman—a desire that exceeded mere sex, a reality that left him slightly confused and very uneasy. But he had a much larger agenda on the verge of coming to fruition, an obsession that had been the driving force in his life dictating everything he had done since the age of fifteen. His plan had to come first, but couldn't he work out some way of having both? Of making love to this incredible woman even though he was deceiving her? And worse yet, knowing he had to continue with that deception until...

He cradled her head against his shoulder as he twined his fingers in her hair. After taking a calming breath, he forced out the words he knew sounded woefully inadequate. "I don't want to play games. In fact, I don't like all those coy little games that some women find so fascinating. I much prefer honesty."

A twinge of guilt stabbed at his consciousness. Yes, he preferred honesty, but he certainly wasn't practicing it at the moment. "I have other things going on in my life right now that are still very unsettled. For the time being I'm not in a position to make any promises. I want to make love to you, but it needs to be something you want, too. And for right now, it needs to be on a no-strings-attached basis. I know that sounds shallow and arrogant even though that's not the type of person I am. But until...well, that's all I can say at this time. If you want me to leave you alone just say so and I'll respect your wishes."

Gable had touched a place in her soul. Even though Lexi didn't know the truth about him or his real identity, she believed his words. He had told her the truth, or at least as much of it as he felt he could. Her earlier decision to not get physically involved with him until she knew who he really was suddenly seemed unimportant. She wrapped her arms around his waist and looked up into his eyes, recognizing both the concern and caution she found there. "I don't like playing all those little games, either. I've never understood why so many women think they need to have the man talk them into doing something they already wanted to do. It's almost as if they feel they're doing something wrong if they admit they have the hots for someone, but if he coerces her into going along then that somehow absolves her of any responsibility and she can claim a clear conscience."

A smile turned the corners of his mouth, part relief, part teasing...and all desire. "Does that mean you're ready to hit the hot tub even though you don't have a swimsuit? And after that..."

"How about reversing that order? The hot tub after..."

The moment his mouth found hers, all the suppressed desires exploded inside her. What a freeing sensation to have everything so above board, at least as far as sex was concerned. But a hint of a troubling cloud continued to linger in the back of her mind. She still had no idea who he really was.

Lexi shoved the concern aside. The secrets, the mysterious happenings, the skeletons...all of it would have to wait. Tonight she had new priorities and the top one was to thoroughly explore the passion that had been bubbling and sizzling between them.

She welcomed his tongue into the dark recesses of her mouth. The meshing of tastes and textures. Her heart raced as the excitement coursed through her veins. Even if it turned out to be nothing more than an incredible interlude, a transitory fling for the duration of her stay on the island, she knew in the very depths of her soul that making love with him would be something to cherish for the rest of her life. Gable Talbot would live in her memory.

Pieces of clothing fell away. They settled into the softness of his king size bed. The very air crackled and sizzled with sexual energy. Lexi's pulse raced and her heart pounded, only this time from excitement rather than fear. She ran her foot along the edge of his calf. A sensual moan escaped her throat when his hand closed over her bare breast. His touch was gentle while at the same time highly stimulating. All thoughts ceased when he drew her puckered nipple into his mouth. Only feelings remained...sensual ripples telling her she wanted much more. She melted into his touch when he inserted a finger between her feminine folds, stroking her into a state of high arousal quicker than anyone else ever had. The spiraling ascent toward orgasm surged through her body.

She wrapped her hand around his girth, marveling at how hard he felt. The awareness caused her fingers to tingle, pushing her over the edge. The ultimate thrill claimed her body, her cry of release muffled when he again captured her mouth with a heated kiss. The delicious taste, the torrid sensations...she wanted more. She also wanted to please him, to give him the pleasure he had given her.

As if able to gauge her needs and desires as long time lovers would, he reached for a condom in the nightstand drawer. She managed a few breathless words. "Let me do that for you." Taking the condom from him, she sensually rolled it on his rigid shaft.

Gable's chest heaved with his labored breathing. Everything about her excited his senses. Her eager responsiveness, the flushed excitement that covered her face as the orgasmic waves claimed her. He nudged his knee between her legs, then settled his body over hers. Slowly delving to the depths of her tunnel, he penetrated the moist heat of her body until he had fully embedded his length. Her muscles closed around him, encasing his shaft in a tight cocoon. He had never been inside a woman who fit him so perfectly or felt so good. Would he be able to keep control long enough to give her another orgasm before he succumbed to the ultimate climax?

They fell into a smooth rhythm, each of his downward strokes met by an upward thrust of her hips. Their bodies moved in harmony as if they had made love many times rather than it being their first time together. The pace increased, consuming each of them in the incendiary atmosphere of hot sex combined with an as yet undefined emotional thread weaving its way through every facet of the moment.

The waves of ecstasy again claimed Lexi. She

wrapped her legs and arms tightly around his body as the contractions clenched inside her followed by the convulsive surges.

Gable gave one last deep plunge. He held her tightly, relishing the hard spasms shuddering through his body. He had never felt more complete than he did at that precise moment. Years of pursuing his personal goal had prevented him from trying to find the one woman who would make his life whole. Had fate intervened by bringing his perfect match to him? How could he juggle the elements of his life so that he could have it all? Was that asking too much? He didn't know the answers and he didn't know what to do. The only thing he did know was that he didn't want to let go of her. He wanted her in his bed and even more important...in his life.

What to do? Somehow he had to make everything work out. But for tonight, all his attention and thoughts would be centered on Lexi. He held her tightly, neither of them saying anything. He forced his breathing into a normal mode, taking a moment every few seconds to place a tender kiss on her cheek or forehead. He wanted to wake in the morning exactly as he hoped to fall asleep...with her in his arms.

But in the interim, renewed stirrings of arousal grabbed his attention.

****

The morning sun streamed in the windows of Lexi's bedroom. She had been awake for about half an hour, but hadn't made any attempt to get out of bed. In spite of the time she and Gable had spent in his hot tub after making love for the second time, her muscles still ached from her tumble into the ravine. She closed her eyes and allowed the inviting sensations of their love making to wash over her. Never had she encountered a man who so completely

Déjà Vu

satisfied her the way he did. He was everything she hoped he would be. And more.

Gable had asked her to stay, to spend the night. And for herself, there was nothing she wanted more at that moment than to wake the next morning in his bed and in his arms. But, as she explained to him, it was not a practical idea. With security people in the house, along with Hank and Dolly making an early morning appearance, it wouldn't do for them to see that she had spent the night in his bedroom. He countered with the argument that it was none of their business. It wasn't like he and Lexi were employer and employee or some other extenuating circumstance. But he reluctantly acquiesced to her point of view saying he didn't want to compromise her reputation.

For her part, that decision was based more on fear than propriety. Certainly not any type of physical fear due to Gable's mysterious background, but rather an emotional fear. If she stayed the night, she would never want to leave. Her thoughts and feelings confused her. Everything seemed to be happening way too fast. It had been a straight forward research assignment, albeit different from her usual assignments. It all sounded so clear cut when she had agreed to go to Skull Island—talk to the owner of the island, find out about his plans for the luxury resort, take pictures, look into the local speculation and gossip about the disappearances.

Then she shook hands with Gable Talbot on the dock and nothing after that moment could be considered simple and straight forward.

Most disturbing of all was her bizarre vision that had become reality in a dramatic and frightening manner. Regardless of what anyone else thought or said, she believed the skeletons were linked to the disappearances. But with three people missing, she wasn't sure exactly which two of them had been buried there. Even though the possibility seemed remote, the skeletons could even have been Winthrop and Jack Stinson leaving the whereabouts of Evelyn a mystery. Not for a moment did she believe Gable's comment about an ancient Native American burial ground. And she knew Gable didn't believe it, either. But again, why would he put forth the deception?

She finally forced her way out of bed and stood in the hot shower until the water soothed her aching muscles. Her bruising wasn't as bad as she thought it would be. After dressing, she walked a couple of doors down the hall to the kitchenette area where she helped herself to coffee, juice, and some fresh pastry Dolly had set out. She had a project for that morning and didn't want to take the time to go to the kitchen and have a full breakfast.

Her brow wrinkled into an involuntary frown as a thought occurred to her. Would Gable think she was purposely avoiding him? That she was upset or angry? She shook her head to clear the troubling thought. She would need to explain it later, but right now she had some computer work to do that would take a while and she needed to get started.

Her priorities had shifted from the research she had been hired to do. Her curiosity had her more fascinated with researching about J.D. Prescott rather than doing research for him. However, not as fascinated as she was with finding out everything she could about Gable Talbot.

Shortly before traveling to Skull Island, she had uncovered a candid snapshot on the internet purported to be the reclusive J.D. Prescott taken five years ago on the city streets of Manhattan. It was a little blurry and he was one face among several. She set about cropping out everything except his head, enlarging that portion of the picture, then cleaning it up and sharpening the image. The end result showed a portrait taken five years ago of a man she believed to be J.D. Prescott. Somewhere in the back of her mind a nagging tickle tried to get her attention, something vaguely familiar about the face, but she couldn't get it to jell.

She had also procured old photographs of Winthrop and Evelyn Hollingsworth and one of Jack Stinson taken the week of the infamous party and had scanned them into her computer before leaving home. She threw herself into the task of aging the images to show what they would look like today, thirty years later. After a few hours she had the pictures of the three missing people aged to what they would probably look like today. She felt her eyes widen as the cold chill spread through her body followed by a tremor of anxiety, then a wave of very real panic.

No wonder the photograph of J.D. Prescott seemed somehow familiar. It may have been Winthrop Hollingsworth's computer aged image she stared at on the screen, but it was the enhanced picture of J.D. Prescott that stared back at her. Truth or nothing more than a colossal coincidence? Could she believe her eyes? Apprehension and elation…a very strange combination…jittered through her until it formed a twisted knot in the pit of her stomach. Could J.D. Prescott really be the long missing Winthrop Hollingsworth? A preposterous notion, but the idea refused to go away. After all these years could Winthrop Hollingsworth still be alive? If so, then he certainly couldn't be one of the skeletons.

She pulled up the manipulated image of Jack Stinson on her computer and studied it. A moment later the certainty popped into her mind. The image from her vision. The face that had progressively evolved into sharper focus each time the vision assaulted her. It exactly matched the picture on the screen. A message from the grave? Jack Stinson trying to contact her? Trying to tell her where his body had been buried? A cold shiver quickly spread across her skin. Her psychic ability had never presented itself to her in such a dramatic manner.

A thousand thoughts and possibilities crashed into each other as they bounced around inside her mind. She had to take things in order, deal with what she could in the best way possible. Was one of the skeletons really Jack Stinson? And her vision, why would it be of a man thirty years older than when he disappeared? If the vision was really Jack Stinson, then shouldn't he look the way he did then? If...well, that would have to wait until the sheriff's lab made the official identification. But for now...

She quickly logged on to the internet and began an in depth search for anything on J.D. Prescott. After a couple of hours of intense work she had not been able to discover one item about him older than thirty years. No record of his birth. No school records. No voter registration. No property ownership. Nothing to indicate the man ever existed before appearing on the scene thirty years ago. Yet the photograph taken five years ago showed a man approximately sixty-years-old which would put him at sixty-five now. That fit in perfectly. Winthrop was thirty-five when he disappeared thirty years ago. The trepidation calmed a little as her racing heart returned to normal.

A computer enhanced photograph of a man believed to be J.D. Prescott and a computer aged photograph of Winthrop Hollingsworth showing them to probably be the same person. A computer aged photograph of Jack Stinson matching the bizarre vision that had assaulted her senses on several occasions since being on Skull Island. But how did all of this fit together?

And how did that relate to Gable? J.D. Prescott

and Gable Talbot. Two men with no past yet somehow entwined in the same mystery if for no other reason than their shared association with Skull Island. Two men hiding behind false identities, each having arrived on the scene with fortunes intact and no trail of where the money came from. Definitely way beyond the scope of mere coincidence. But what did it mean? Winthrop and Evelyn didn't have any children, but could Winthrop have had a son? Could Gable be an illegitimate child seeking his rightful share of the family money? But if so, where did the fortune Gable already possessed come from? Being able to pay ten million dollars cash for an island indicated a sizeable fortune. Maybe it was really Hollingsworth money being used to keep the family secrets from surfacing. But with the discovery of the skeletons, that was no longer a viable situation.

Too many confusing possibilities. And none of them felt right to her.

One thing she needed to do before the news became common knowledge...she needed to email Prescott and tell him about the discovery of the skeletons so he would believe all her efforts were concentrated on his requirements. In fact, she should have done it yesterday. She would tell him about being caught in the mudslide, the traumatic experience had sent her to bed with a concussion and other minor injuries, with this being her first opportunity to contact him.

An amused chuckle surprised her as it escaped her throat. *It's going to be interesting to see his response to this little tidbit of information.*

After sending the email, she turned her thoughts to the next item on her list—confronting Gable with what she had discovered about him and demanding some answers. Whatever he was hiding might keep him from making promises or offering a commitment of some sort, but after last night he owed her some answers if nothing else. And she wanted those answers. She wanted...no, she *needed*...to know his true identity. She could not continue to be intimately involved with a man who had been deceiving her.

Lexi set about gathering together her information and organizing her thoughts. It was already lunch time. She had stayed in her room all morning, but now she needed to confront Gable. They had to find a private place where she could—

The loud knock on her door startled her out of her thoughts, followed by a jolt of adrenalin. A little shiver of anxiety accompanied the unwelcome possibility that immediately popped into her head. Could it be Brian Cookson again? She recalled the way he had stared at her from the top of the ravine, not making any effort to help her until Hank and Dolly arrived. Had he been contemplating doing her some harm? But why? And why had he been in the area when she fell into the ravine, close enough to hear her calls for help?

With everything that happened, plus what she had discovered that morning from her research, her impressions about him being dangerous were all the more disturbing. Then another unpleasant thought hit her.

Perhaps she was not the only person on the island being paid by J.D. Prescott.

Or Winthrop Hollingsworth.

Déjà Vu

Chapter Seven

When Gable didn't receive any response to his knock, he knocked again. It had taken all his will power to keep from going to her room when she didn't show up for breakfast. He had attempted to work in his office, but finally gave up trying to concentrate after he read an email for the third time and still didn't know what it said. Was she all right? Had some latent injuries surfaced as a result of her fall? Had she decided to stay in bed and rest? Or worse? Had she physically been unable to get out of bed?

Then his real fear finally penetrated that wall he had put up to keep it away. Had she developed second thoughts about them making love? Was this her way of telling him she regretted her decision? That possibility bothered him more than anything. Physical injuries would heal. Emotional exhaustion from her ordeal at the ravine would pass. But her rejection would surely touch him in every way possible, destroying any possible plans for a future that would include Alexandra Caldwell as part of his life.

One way or the other, he needed to know why she had chosen to remain secluded in her room all morning. The anxiety churned inside him to the point where he could not stand it any longer. He called to her through the door. "Lexi...are you in there? Are you okay?" As he raised his hand to knock again, the door swung open.

The expression on her face confused him. At

first it showed caution, then quickly changed to relief when her gaze settled on him. He entered her room, closing the door behind him. Almost as an involuntary action, he pulled her into his embrace. She felt good in his arms as if she belonged there. "You didn't come to breakfast and stayed in your room all morning. Dolly has lunch ready and you're still in your room. I've been worried about you, but didn't know if I should disturb you or not. I didn't want to intrude if you preferred..." His words trailed off when he realized he had been on the verge of babbling. He brushed a tender kiss across her lips. "I know you told me not to ask you this again, but I can't help it. Are you all right?"

The little tremor of apprehension said it wasn't her health that troubled him. "I was afraid that maybe...uh...I mean, after last night I wondered if you..." He gave up trying to articulate his true concerns. For someone who could manifest a commanding presence and confident demeanor whenever he needed it, he had suddenly turned into an inarticulate bumbler incapable of expressing himself in an understandable manner.

"Are you trying to ask me if I'm suffering from *morning after* regrets?" Her voice teased as she slipped her arms around his waist and rested her head against his shoulder. Then her tone turned serious. "No...no regrets on my part."

The sigh of relief that shuddered through his body reverberated to her. But that didn't mean there wasn't something very important that they needed to discuss. She drew in a calming breath, held it for a couple of seconds, then slowly exhaled. And now was as good a time as any, in the privacy of her room where no one could see or hear them.

A discussion that couldn't wait any longer.

Truth that must be brought out in the open.

She reluctantly pulled away from his embrace.

Being in his arms kept her from thinking clearly. His mere touch clouded her thoughts with emotion. "We do need to talk, but it's not about last night." Caution immediately filled his eyes, the sight sending a flicker of anxiety rippling through her body.

"Okay..." His voice held as much wariness as did his gaze.

"I'm not sure where or how to begin."

He grasped her hand, but she pulled away from him. "Please don't do that. This is difficult enough without the physical contact." Her nerves stretched to a tautly strung edginess. "I guess the thing to do is just say it outright."

She made eye contact with him and held it for several seconds as she gathered what she hoped were the proper words. "I've checked on some of the people I've encountered since beginning my research into the disappearances and I've come up with some things I can't explain." She sucked in another steadying breath, held it for several seconds as she stared at the floor, then slowly let it out. It didn't do anything to lessen the uneasiness churning inside her. "First and foremost...uh, first on my list is..." she looked up and caught another moment of eye contact with him, "is you."

"Me?" His eyes widened in surprise followed by the flicker of anxiety that danced across his face.

She tried to read his tone and expression, but couldn't get a handle on his thoughts. There was nothing for her to do other than tell him what she found...or in his case, didn't find. She paused as she gathered her courage, then blurted out the words. "Gable Talbot didn't exist before five years ago." She didn't sound as confident and in control as she hoped she would. "Four and a half years ago you paid ten million dollars cash for Skull Island without any indication of where the money came from."

She attempted to force a calm to the knotted lump in the pit of her stomach. As much as she tried, she could not keep the quaver out of her voice. "I keep asking myself the same questions. Who...who are you? Where did you come from? Why was it so important for you to own this island that you paid more than it was worth in order to possess it? Surely not just to open a resort. There are plenty of places where you could have purchased very desirable land for a lot less than ten million dollars."

Gable closed his eyes for a moment, his face clearly displaying the anxiety her comments caused. His words were tentative at best, conveying his discomfort with the topic. "And did you come up with any answers?"

"No...at least not any that satisfy me. I even went so far as to toy with the notion that you might be a member of the Hollingsworth family, possibly Winthrop's illegitimate son, and you paid for the island with Hollingsworth money. Then I dismissed that theory because...well, it just didn't feel right to me, didn't make a lot of sense. So, now I'm asking you." She forced out the words that tried to choke off in her throat. "Who is Gable Talbot? Who are you?"

He turned and stared out the window, his gaze falling on the ocean without really focusing on it. What to do. How much to tell her. He had known the time would come when he had to confide the truth to her, especially after they spent an incredible night making love. A night that had a remarkable impact on his life. A night that confirmed his involvement with her had moved beyond the physical to encompass the emotional as well. But he had not been prepared for her to confront him the very next day and certainly not with the knowledge of his deception about his identity.

Divulge his entire plan to her? Confess his true identity while holding back the details of his

Déjà Vu

scheme? He had never felt so torn between two opposing ends of one reality. Even as a teenager he knew what had to be done. For twenty-five years he had pursued a single-minded course of action and long range plan aimed at one, and only one, conclusion. A plan that included his one and only long time ally and confidant.

And now he stood there, staring out the window and wondering what to do. He tried to shake off his rapidly growing apprehension. He had no option other than to trust her with the truth. At least part of it...for the time being. He turned to face her, but stayed more than arm's length away. He could not allow his desire for her to cloud his thinking and touching her would do just that.

A sigh of resignation escaped his throat. "You're putting me in a position I wasn't quite ready to accept in spite of the fact that I've given it considerable thought over the last day or so. I wanted to be honest with you." He tried to calm his rattled nerves, but without much success. "What I'm about to tell you must be kept in the strictest of confidence. The seriousness of what's going on here...the importance of all this can't be emphasized too much. There cannot be any exceptions. I need to have your absolute promise of discretion and complete secrecy."

"I promise." Her words had been barely above a whisper, her expression one of total confusion.

He sucked in a steadying breath. Things had gone too far and now he couldn't turn back. He had to tell her. A quick glance at the floor as he rallied his determination, then he allowed the words he had promised not to say. "You're right. Gable Talbot didn't exist prior to five years ago. My name was Jonathon Stinson before I had it legally changed. I'm...Jack Stinson's son."

Her eyes widened in shock and the color drained

from her face. "You...you're Jack Stinson's son?"

Had she heard him correctly? Her entire body trembled from the emotional turmoil coursing through her veins. She fell backward into a chair in stunned silence. Her mind refused to focus, refused to process the information. She stared at him in disbelief as she shook her head in an attempt to clear the fuzziness.

Gable rushed toward her, kneeling next to her chair. His voice carried genuine concern. "Lexi...are you all right?"

He grabbed her hand and held it to his chest as he made an unsuccessful attempt at a teasing tone of voice. "I know. You told me not to ask you that again." Then the seriousness returned. "But you looked like you'd seen a ghost. I'm sure what I told you is not what you were expecting to hear, but I had no idea it would have such an adverse affect."

"I'm...I'm okay." She tried to force a smile, but only managed a slight upward turn at the corners of her mouth. Her tremors escalated to the point of being almost out of control. "I'm not sure what to say, how to respond to that. I suspected you might have some sort of connection to what happened here thirty years ago even though I couldn't imagine what it might be, but the possibility of you being Jack Stinson's son never entered my mind."

"As for the money to buy this island...well, I started an internet company and sold it five years ago for a considerable amount of money. The fortune is mine and I came by it honestly. It's given me the freedom to concentrate all my efforts on proving that my father did not murder anyone. It's my belief that Winthrop murdered his wife and my father was nothing more than a scapegoat. From everything I've gathered over the years, I've determined that my father was not having an affair with Evelyn. In fact, I discovered he didn't even particularly like her or

Déjà Vu

Winthrop. He considered both of them to be pretentious, self-centered snobs. His presence on the island was part of his job and nothing more."

"What about your mother? Where is she?"

"My mother died three years ago. Even though my parents were divorced, she never believed the gossip and rumors about my father. She lived long enough to see me put a carefully thought out plan into play starting with the purchase of Skull Island." He paused as a moment of regret flashed across his face. "I only wish she could have lived to see my father's name cleared."

He set his jaw in a hard line of determination. "And I intend to see it happen no matter how long it takes or how much it costs."

He cocked is head and leveled a quizzical look at her. "Perhaps you can answer a question for me. What made you suspect I had some sort of involvement in an event that happened thirty years ago? I was only a child, barely nine years old. There was never anything mentioned that said there were any children involved in the events of that night. Winthrop and Evelyn never had any children and I lived with my mother in California at the time and had never been to Skull Island."

"I…well," a nervous jitter told her how uncomfortable she was with his question, but probably no more so than he had been with her probing and prying. "I sort of have this psychic ability…visions about things, but I don't know how to control it or properly interpret what I see."

He stared at her as if not believing what she had said. "Psychic abilities?"

She bristled at what she interpreted as his condescending manner. Was he making fun of her? "You asked the question and that's my answer." Her words came out with an edge of defensiveness she had not been able to control. "If you don't believe me, then there's nothing I can say that will change your mind."

"Whoa...pull in your claws. I didn't say anything about not believing you. As Shakespeare wrote in Hamlet, *There are more things in heaven and earth, Horatio, than are dreamt of in your philosophy.* I'm not denying the existence of psychic abilities. I'm just surprised at your answer. I've never met anyone before who claimed to be...uh, I mean anyone who is psychic."

"Well..." A moment of sheepish embarrassment claimed her. "I...uh, didn't mean to jump to conclusions—"

"It's all right. We both seem to have some surprises in us. Have you always had these psychic abilities? Does this run in your family?"

A moment of sadness washed over her. "I don't have any immediate family any more. I'm an only child. My parents were killed in an automobile accident eight years ago." She managed to force an upbeat manner in an attempt to change the mood. "As far as my psychic visions...you're the first to know. I started having them when I was a teenager. I thought something was wrong with me so I never told anyone about them. Maybe if I had confided in someone, had found others with the same type of abilities, I could have gained some viable knowledge in that area. But, that wasn't the case. So, I'm stuck between knowing something and not understanding what it is."

"Do you know what triggered your psychic senses about me?"

She forced her attention back to the matter at hand. "When I arrived and we shook hands on the dock, a vision popped into my mind. A horrifying image of mud sliding toward me and skeletons. It repeated several times. I didn't have any idea what it meant but it seemed to tie you, the island, and my

Déjà Vu

research together." A cold shiver swept across her skin. Her words came out barely above a whisper. "Yesterday that vision became a frightening reality."

Gable couldn't maintain his distance from her any longer. He stepped in close and folded her in his embrace, holding her close to him. "I can't begin to imagine the terror you must have experienced when you saw that wall of mud sliding toward you, then the skeletons..." If making love hadn't confirmed how much he wanted to pursue a true relationship with her, then the sharing of deeply held secrets sealed his fate. No matter how his quest played out in the arena of real life, he could not allow her to be lost in the process.

She wrapped her arms around his waist as he nestled her head against his shoulder. Neither of them spoke, each content to sway gently back and forth in each other's arms. Several minutes passed before either of them made any attempt to break the spell binding them together.

Gable brushed a soft kiss across Lexi's lips. "I told Dolly I was fetching you for lunch. She's going to have a fit if we don't show up in the kitchen right away."

"I am hungry. I didn't really have any breakfast."

"I know."

"There's more..." She paused, as if uncertain about whether or not to continue. "I need to show you what I've been working on this morning. You aren't the only one whose background I was curious about. I really think you need to see what I found as soon as possible. I can show you now," she waved her arm indicating her laptop computer. "If you have some time."

He stepped back and studied her for a moment. "Would it be better if we had lunch in my office? We can shut the door and be assured of complete privacy. That will allow us to eat as we talk."

"Give me a moment to gather my work materials."

A few minutes later, they headed toward his office. Gable carried the tote bag containing her papers and laptop computer. While she set up her computer, he went to the kitchen and brought back a lunch tray.

Once locked behind his office door, she hooked her laptop to his printer and printed out the computer aged pictures, then explained to him what she had been doing. "I procured photographs of the principals involved in the case—Winthrop, Evelyn, and Jack...uh, your father—and aged them to what they would look like today. Here is what I ended up with." She placed two of the photographs on the table. "This is Winthrop and Evelyn." She put a third photograph on the table next to the other two. "I located a candid photograph of your father that had been taken during the party preparations. This is what he would look like today."

Gable picked up the photographs of Winthrop and Evelyn and studied them. Their faces were ones he knew well. They had been burned into his mind. "It's very interesting seeing them as they would look now." He replaced the photographs on the table.

"In my research I had come across a candid snapshot, a paparazzi type photo taken on the streets of Manhattan five years ago that's supposed to be J.D. Prescott. As you had mentioned when I first arrived on the island, I also couldn't figure out how the research information he wanted would fit in with the type of books he writes. That, combined with my suspicions about you, led me to look into Prescott's life and see what I could find. I wanted to know what connection he had to you, why he wanted to know about you specifically and what you had planned for the island."

Nervous anxiety churned in the pit of Lexi's stomach. Was she doing the right thing in sharing what she found? She had never felt so sure of anything while at the same time being so uncertain. Making love with him had thoroughly captured her emotions, but that did not make it prudent to forsake her logic and common sense. Something very unsettling was happening on Skull Island and she didn't understand her part in it. Was she a willing accomplice or an unwitting dupe? Had she gotten too close to the truth? Could her life be in danger?

One thing for sure, if she wanted to leave there was no way off the island without someone else's help. The only remote possibility she had for any assistance would be to call the sheriff's office on her cell phone, but even that was speculative at best. Gable and Deputy Lansing had appeared to be friends, at least enough so that they referred to each other by first name. Gable's adamant statements about intruders being arrested for trespassing had been taken very seriously by the sheriff's department to the point where they were willing to send a boat in a storm to pick up the reporter. Any call she made for help would most likely not be kept confidential.

Gable's voice interrupted her wandering thoughts. "And what did you find?"

"Huh?" Her mind raced to grab hold of what they had been talking about before more pressing matters occupied her thoughts.

"What did you find when you looked into Prescott's life?"

Where had all her sudden doubts come from? She was already too far into things to suddenly shut down. She gathered her resolve. "I isolated his face from the rest of the photograph, cleaned up the image, and enlarged it. This is what I ended up with." She placed the photo of J.D. Prescott next to the computer aged photo of Winthrop Hollingsworth. She heard his quick intake of breath as his eyes widened in shock. He picked up the two photos and studied them.

She tried to control the quaver in her voice. "My first thought matched the expression on your face...the two people shown in the photos are the same person." She shot him a questioning look. "What do you think?"

The words came out as not much more than a whisper while he continued to stare at the two photos. "Winthrop Hollingsworth really is alive and well. I've always believed it. I felt it in the depths of my soul. It's the one thing that helped keep me focused on my goal all these years, knowing that I would eventually be able to prove it. And now I finally know where he is and who he turned himself into."

Gable looked up at Lexi, capturing a moment of eye contact. She saw the pain in his eyes, the anguish that covered his features telling of a deep emotional wound. "We don't need to wait for the official identification to tell us that the two skeletons are Evelyn Hollingsworth...and my father. Winthrop murdered both of them, then disappeared and created a new identity for himself."

The pain covering his face touched her as nothing else ever had. More than anything she wanted to comfort him, to let him know he was not alone. She tentatively touched his cheek, then slipped her arms around his waist and leaned her head against his shoulder. "I'm sorry. I shouldn't have hit you with this without some words of warning. I wasn't thinking beyond my initial surprise and the excitement of discovery when I realized the two photos depicted the same person...or at least they appeared to be the same person. I should have—"

"There's no reason for you to apologize." He put his arms around her and rested his cheek against the top of her head. "You've provided me with some important missing pieces that I might have eventually connected, but without your help it could have taken me a long time. Thank you."

Then the realization popped into her mind. Why hadn't he picked up the computer aged photograph of Jack Stinson? Surely he would find it interesting to see what his father would look like today. Had his statement about being Jack Stinson's son been the truth or a ruse to gain her confidence? Had she played into his hands by showing him what she had found, especially connecting the altered photograph of Winthrop with the candid picture of J.D. Prescott?

No. She shoved away the inappropriate thought. His pain was real, the emotion genuine. One of the skeletons was Jack Stinson…his father.

"I don't know what your intentions are, but you mentioned having put an existing plan into action starting with the purchase of Skull Island. I want to help you. If everything that's happened proves to be exactly what it appears to be, that means J.D. Prescott used me for his own purposes. That gives me a stake in all of this. He didn't need research for a book. I think he wanted to know whether there was any danger of your resort plans accidentally uncovering the bodies. If he hired a private detective, that would create suspicions. But using a researcher to compile information for his next book wouldn't stir the same type of curiosity."

She stepped back from his embrace and looked up into the depths of his green eyes. "What do you want me to do? The only communication I've had with Prescott since my arrival here is an email I sent him first thing this morning telling him about the discovery of the skeletons."

She saw a moment of displeasure dart across his

face, but she put a stop to it before he could say anything. "It was only a matter of time before what happened would be on the news. By emailing him with the information, I gave the appearance that I'm still doing the job he's paying me to do. Had I not reported to him, within twenty-four hours he would have known about it anyway compounded by the fact that I could not deny knowledge of the incident since I was the one who ended up in the ravine with the skeletons."

His expression softened. "You're right. You did what needed to be done."

"There must be some way we can use this to lure him here to the island. If you could confront him face-to-face..."

"That, in itself, wouldn't accomplish anything. I never met Winthrop Hollingsworth and coming right out and confronting him wouldn't have any impact on what needs to happen. I'd be accusing J.D. Prescott of being Winthrop and he'd deny it. I have no proof...yet. He'd relate to me as the person who currently owns this island and might even be able to give me a sketchy story idea that would explain his interest in the research he hired you to do."

"But what about fingerprints? Surely Winthrop's fingerprints would be somewhere. The police could take Prescott's and compare them. That would be proof that they are the same person."

"The police would need some sort of proof, at least a form of probable cause, before they would try to force Prescott to give his fingerprints. And that assumes there is some sort of official record of Winthrop's fingerprints for the comparison."

A sigh of resignation surrounded her words. "You're right."

"Confronting him without proof wouldn't get us any closer to proving he's Winthrop or that he committed two murders that night. The only thing it

Déjà Vu

would do is put him on full alert that his secret wasn't as safe as he thought. In fact, it could put us...especially you...in physical danger."

She nodded her head. "I see what you mean."

"However, getting him here to the island is something that could play into a revised version of my plan. All we need to do is figure out something powerful enough to lure him here, something so important that a self-determined recluse would want to leave the security of his home and anonymity and expose himself to the scrutiny of others in a place where he did not have control of the situation and didn't have anyone answerable to him who could do his bidding. If we could come up with something—"

"I don't think that's true."

Surprise covered his features. "What's not true?"

"The part about him being isolated here without help. I think maybe...I mean..."

A hint of a teasing grin tugged at the corners of his mouth. "Stop doing that."

"Doing what?"

"Talking like you're not sure of what you're saying. I find you very astute and observant. Stop trying to downplay those qualities. Never pretend to be less than what you are."

"That's not what I'm doing. I really am uncertain about what I was going to say. It's only a feeling, nothing more."

A look of uncertainty crossed his face, as if he didn't quite know how to respond to what she had said. "Another psychic vision?"

"No, not a vision. Actually, more of a psychic hunch. I don't think I'm the only person on this island at the behest of J.D. Prescott. How much of a background check did you do on Brian Cookson? Did you check him out or just accept his application?"

"Brian?" Gable furrowed his brow in a moment of confusion. "You think Brian has some connection

119

to all of this beyond being an employee here?"

"As I said, it's only a hunch. When you first introduced me to him and we shook hands, a bad feeling telegraphed itself to me. It said Brian was a very dangerous man. I had the feeling again when he came to the door of my room ostensibly to tell me dinner was almost ready and to escort me to the dining room at your request. Did you ask him to do that?"

"No..." His voice became wary, his manner cautious as if not quite knowing where the conversation was headed. "I didn't send him to your room."

"And yesterday afternoon, he was the first one to arrive at the ravine. He stood there staring down at me, not moving or making any effort to help. For a moment I actually feared that he intended to do me harm. It was only a few seconds later when we heard Dolly's voice that Brian finally reacted and decided to be helpful."

A clearly agitated Gable grabbed her shoulders and held her. His voice contained controlled anger. "Did he threaten you, Lexi?"

"No, nothing like that. He didn't do anything. It was only a feeling, a psychic impression. Call it women's intuition, if that's more comfortable for you."

He loosened his hold on her. "My background check on him wasn't that thorough. I checked out his references and that was about it. Everyone gave him high marks for being conscientious, dependable, and a good worker." He sucked in a calming breath. "This is all very strange."

"Yes." She slowly shook her head as she tried to put some semblance of order to her thoughts. "And becoming stranger by the minute."

"We have several pieces of this enigma. You've provided me with a new avenue of investigation. I've done every kind of check I could think of going forward from the time of the disappearances, both computer check and having a detective dig into it. I checked every trail I could find in trying to discover where Winthrop would have gone. I even speculated about Evelyn and Winthrop both being alive and having perpetrated the entire hoax to cover some bigger crime and killing my father because he accidentally stumbled across their plan. Everything came up as a dead end. But now...thanks to your efforts...I can trace from today and go back to the disappearances. I can start with J.D. Prescott. I'll also recheck Brian's references to see if any of those companies have a connection to Prescott."

"I tried to check on Prescott. Every avenue went back thirty years, then disappeared into thin air. Everything I dug up said he appeared thirty years ago with fortune already in hand. We now know why, but how do we prove it?"

"We follow the money, not the man. Winthrop had to make arrangements for a great deal of money to be available to him in a manner that wouldn't raise any questions or create suspicion. The money had to come from the Hollingsworth business conglomerate and it most likely would have been a transaction that he personally dealt with to avoid questions from accounting clerks or financial people. Thirty years ago the world was not so highly computerized. False identification wasn't that difficult to get, especially when you could afford to buy the very best. His new identity and his financial status had to be in place prior to the night of the costume party. Something this elaborate would have taken time to work out all the details. It was not an impulsive act or last minute decision. It was a carefully constructed plan."

Lexi stared at him for a moment as she turned the words over in her mind. "You're very good at this, extrapolating a viable sounding theory from a few bits of miscellaneous information."

"I like solving puzzles. It's the way my mind works. It goes to the logical. That's why I'm so good with computers and was able to build an internet company worth a great deal of money."

"You have logic and I have psychic visions." Her words sounded sheepish even to her own ears, almost as if she was embarrassed to have said them.

He took her hand in his, slowly lacing their fingers together. His voice turned soft, his words covered in intimacy. "Sounds to me like a good combination. What do you think?"

She made eye contact with him, holding his gaze for what seemed like eternity before answering. The words came out of her mouth before she could stop them. "I think you might possibly be right."

The moment hung in the air, neither of them saying anything. Lexi finally broke the spell binding them together. "But this is neither the time nor place."

His words were cloaked in soft emotion. "I know."

Déjà Vu

Chapter Eight

"Damn! I sure didn't expect this." Gable read the printed email for the second time, then handed it back to Lexi. "I'll say one thing for Prescott, he's crafty."

"According to the time on it, he just sent it to me about ten minutes ago. That means he came up with this plan in less than eight hours from the time I emailed him this morning. But a mind that could dream up those novels he writes is capable of all kinds of things."

"Yes...things like a double murder that went unsolved for thirty years because there was never any proof that anyone had even been killed. Things like creating a new identity and totally reinventing himself."

Lexi shot Gable a sidelong glance. "Well, he's not the only one who successfully reinvented himself."

He touched his fingertip to her nose while suppressing a grin. "Point taken."

"What do you want to do about this email from Prescott? Even though he says it's a request, it sure reads like an order. He wants you to host a lavish costume party identical to the one the night of the disappearances as a combined publicity event for his upcoming book and the island's proposed resort. He even wants the same guests invited who attended the original party including the descendents of those who have died. And then there's this part about him using the occasion to make a major announcement that will solve the thirty-year-old mystery surrounding the disappearance of Evelyn and Winthrop Hollingsworth. I can't imagine him admitting that J.D. Prescott is really the missing Winthrop Hollingsworth. What in the world could he be up to?"

Gable glanced at the clock on his desk. They had been busy all afternoon and now it was nearly dinner time. "Brian comes on shift in half an hour. If we want to keep him from being overly suspicious, we need to vacate my office and be seen separately."

"Did you find anything on the references Brian used on his résumé? The ones who gave him a glowing report?"

"Yes. It took some serious digging through corporate structures, but it turns out that all three companies are connected to Prescott even though he's not officially listed on any of the corporate paperwork or roster of officers. I didn't have enough time to crack the list of stockholders, but I suspect he also holds a significant block of shares in each of the companies. But the telling piece is that Prescott was a silent partner in a security business Brian used to own. So," he paused a moment to pull her into his arms, "your *psychic hunch* was right on the money."

Gable brushed a soft kiss across Lexi's lips, then captured her mouth with a heated kiss that nearly took her breath away. All thought of work evaporated in an incendiary flash. It took several seconds before she pulled her composure together and broke off the kiss. "We don't have time for this right now. Brian will be on duty shortly. We have to get a plan together."

"You're right." He placed another quick kiss on her lips then turned his attention to the business at hand. "The original party was a lavish Halloween costume event. That night a rainstorm complete with thunder and lightning swept across the island.

Déjà Vu

The power went out. It was during the blackout that Winthrop and Evelyn disappeared. It was later determined that the power outage had been rigged and one of the island's small motor boats came up missing. The prevailing theory said my father turned off the power to create confusion while he murdered Winthrop and Evelyn, then used the boat to get off the island and disappear, most likely taking the bodies with him and dumping them at sea.

"That's a lot for one man to accomplish on his own. Especially turning off the power then having only a couple of minutes at the most to make his way in the dark to grab both Winthrop and Evelyn from a ballroom filled with people. And all of that without any assistance in physically subduing them yet neither of them called for help. I, personally, never did believe that was even possible let alone probable. I've been able to verify that no one saw my father at any time during the afternoon before the party. I think he was already dead. Winthrop rigged the electricity earlier and grabbed Evelyn when the lights went out at the predetermined time. Knowing exactly when the ballroom would be plunged into darkness, he could have maneuvered Evelyn to the French doors moments before. He probably already had my father's body stored in some secret place and all he had to do was put Evelyn's body there, too, and go into hiding until things calmed down and he could bury them, then escape."

"That all makes sense. In fact, it's the first thing I've come across that really does make complete sense. But what do you want me to tell Prescott about this party thing?"

"Don't tell him anything yet. Let him sit around and wonder if I'm going to take the bait. We can't let him call the shots."

Lexi glanced at the clock. "I'd better gather my

stuff and take it back to my room before Brian sees me." She put all her papers and her laptop in the tote bag, then reached for the doorknob. Gable's hand on her shoulder stopped her before she could open the door. She shot him a curious glance.

"Be careful. If Brian Cookson is on Prescott's payroll, then he's most likely watching your every move even more than mine. As far as anyone knows, I'm just the guy who bought the island. But you...that's a different story. You have a direct connection to Prescott. Brian would have contacted Prescott right away about the skeletons, probably when he went to change his clothes right after Bud arrived. That gave Prescott additional time to work out his plan, not just from the time you emailed him. In fact, it might be a good idea for you to keep your research material here rather than your room. I can lock the papers in my safe and transfer your sensitive computer files about me and Prescott to my computer. You can work on your laptop in here using your routine research information. I keep my office locked at all times, but I can give you a key."

They each recognized the offer of a key to his office as more than a temporary solution to a possible problem. It was the same as her willingly handing her research information to him. It conveyed a genuine level of trust, one born from a newly forged emotional connection between them.

"That's a good idea." She handed the tote bag to Gable. "I'll go to my room and get ready for dinner." Taking the initiative, she placed a quick kiss on his lips. "I'll see you in the kitchen."

Lexi glanced around as she left Gable's office, thankful that she didn't see anyone...especially Brian. A bit of a grin tugged at the corners of her mouth. Gable's decision to let Prescott wait for a while before answering his email amused her. Everything she had heard about J.D. Prescott in publishing circles said he was a control freak. And now that they knew his true identity, it confirmed his need to have control of everything. One of the many facets of Winthrop Hollingsworth's life that had repeatedly been mentioned in the press was his need to control. It gave them a tool to use against him, something to work in their favor. Take away that control. Make him function on their terms.

At the end of the hall, she rounded the corner headed toward the glass walkway that connected the back wing to the house. Her heart beat jumped and she came to an abrupt halt. The hard jolt of anxiety hit her. Brian stood blocking her way. Was it coincidental or had he been waiting for her? She tried to force a calm to her voice.

"Good evening, Brian."

"Good evening, Miss Caldwell. I was just looking for Mr. Talbot. Have you seen him?"

"Gable?" *Be careful what you say. Don't talk too much. Don't offer any information. Don't try to explain something when there's nothing to explain.* "Not lately. Have you checked the kitchen?"

Brian pointedly stared at her as if he knew she had lied. Or was that her own guilty conscience? "Yes. Dolly said he picked up a lunch tray for two, but that was a few hours ago and she hadn't seen him since then."

A welcome relief settled over her when she spotted Gable out of the corner of her eye. She pointed toward the enclosed courtyard. "Isn't that him over there by the swimming pool?"

A look of surprise covered Brian's face when he turned and saw Gable checking the chemical balance of the water. "Uh…yes. Well, he looks busy. I'll catch him later."

Lexi hurried toward her room, thankful to be away from Brian. Now that she knew more about him, about his background, the danger she felt from him made sense. She couldn't put him on alert by letting on that they suspected him of something. Whatever Gable planned...a slight frown tugged at her forehead. Even though Gable had trusted her with a key to his office, he had not shared any of his plan with her. A sigh of resignation said all she could do was wait until he was ready to confide in her.

****

Lexi snuggled into Gable's arms as he stroked his fingers across her bare skin. Making love had touched him even deeper than it had the previous night. It had solidified what he already knew. Not only were they involved together in untangling a thirty-year-old murder mystery, the involvement was emotional as well as physical. In a dramatically short amount of time she had become very important to him. Perhaps too important? He chased the dark thought away before it could go any further. He knew that was his fear talking, not reality.

His agenda had taken a sudden turn into the fast lane since the arrival of Lexi and knowledge of what she had discovered. Everything made complete sense now. He had all the elements. He needed only to assemble them into the final picture. What had looked like it could be another year in coming to fruition now loomed on the horizon where he could almost reach out and touch it. The culmination of his hard work and driven obsession could now be numbered in days rather than months. And once he had cleared his father's name and seen to it that Winthrop Hollingsworth was exposed so the law could deal with him, he would be able to give his full attention to Lexi.

The phone call he made a few hours ago put another step of his plan into action. How the final step played out would depend on J.D. Prescott's response to Gable's decision about recreating the costume party from the night of the disappearances.

Lexi shifted position, drawing his attention back to the present. He placed a tender kiss on her forehead while tightening his hold on her. "Are you awake?" He whispered the words so not to disturb her if she was asleep. He also didn't want her to return to her own room as she had done last night. The idea of waking in the morning with her sleeping next to him felt very right.

"Mmmm…yes, I'm awake."

"I've been thinking about Brian. We don't want him to know that we're on to him and his connection with Prescott."

"We also don't know if he's even aware of Prescott's true identity."

"Right. So I think the best thing for me to do is put Brian on the day shift so there are other people around when he's on duty. That should limit his movements. The night shift gives him too many opportunities to snoop. Someone tried to access my computer. At the time, I wasn't sure who did it." He shot her an embarrassed grin. "I even wondered if it might have been you."

Lexi raised up on one elbow, surprise covering her face. "Me?"

"For me, you were the unknown factor that had been introduced into the equation. While you were doing research into my background, I was suspicious of you."

"Well…" she emitted a soft chuckle, "since you put it that way I can't disagree with your logic."

He pulled her back into his embrace. "Now I'm sure it must have been Brian. That means he was able to get into my office. He wasn't successful with the computer, but that doesn't mean he won't try again. By putting him on days, he won't have any excuse to be in the halls of my house at night. I've also installed some added security devices in my office and a couple of other places as a precaution."

"I'm glad you've taken some steps to keep closer tabs on Brian. He frightens me. Even this evening after I left your office...I told you about running into him in the hall." A shiver darted across her skin reminding her of the anxiety her brief encounter with Brian had caused. She placed a tender kiss on Gable's chest while splaying her fingers across his thigh as much to seek out the comfort of the physical contact as to initiate lovemaking.

"I was going to tell you about my decision concerning Prescott's request to recreate the original party," his voice turned to a husky whisper, "but I think it can wait until we finish this."

He cupped her breast and teased her nipple with the tip of his tongue until it puckered into a taut bud. His touch excited her senses as no one else ever had. She wanted to know about his plan, but as he said...it could wait. Right now she wanted more of him.

And that was her last conscious thought. His mouth claimed hers in a passion-filled kiss. Tremors of excitement assaulted her senses when he slipped his finger between her feminine folds and sensually stroked her core. Her breathing quickened as the delicious sensations coursed through her body. Her fingers wrapped around his rigid shaft. His groan of pleasure reached her ears, sending her level of arousal soaring. Waves of incendiary delight crashed through her body causing her to cry out in delicious release.

Gable reached for a condom. A minute later he positioned himself between her legs and slowly entered her. She gasped as the intense sensation filled her. Every time he touched her, every place he touched her, left her panting for more. Everything about him pushed her to the pinnacle. He guided her into a smooth rhythm that quickly escalated as the heat built to a fever pitch. She tightened her legs and arms around him as the orgasmic convulsions claimed her again. Seconds later his body shuddered as his climax meshed with hers.

They held each other for what seemed like a long time, neither of them wanting to move or break the magical spell binding them together. She reveled in the closeness and warmth she felt with him, something she didn't want to ever lose. Their lives had become entwined on several levels ranging from the passion of their lovemaking to the dangers of the mystery unfolding around them.

Thirty years ago two people were murdered. The murderer had escaped detection...until now. But how to get him into the open, prove that J.D. Prescott and Winthrop Hollingsworth were one and the same and that he killed his wife and Jack Stinson?

"Stay with me all night." Gable's voice interrupted her thoughts.

"Mmmm...I'd like to, but isn't that a little dangerous? What if someone sees me leaving your room in the morning? Especially if that person is Brian?"

A sigh of resignation escaped his throat. "You're right. When I change Brian's shift, I'll have him working from nine in the morning until six in the evening. That won't interfere with what happens here first thing in the morning." He brushed a kiss across her lips. "That will allow us our privacy in addition to keeping Brian where I can watch him."

"I like that." She snuggled her body against his for a moment, then sat up. "But until then, I need to get back to my room before it gets any later. I imagine Brian does his snooping after midnight."

"Let's stage a little show for his benefit. Instead of you going back to your room, let's go to the game room and play a little pool. We'll make sure he knows we're there, then I can check in at the security room to make sure he stays put while you go to your room so you won't be confronted by him in the hallway again."

Gable wrinkled his forehead into a slight frown as he locked eye contact with her. "I don't want to worry you, but it might be a good idea if you hook the back of a chair under the door knob in your room to make sure no one can get in...something more than just locking the door."

Her eyes widened in surprise. "Do you think I'm in danger?"

"I'm sure you're not, but you did say Brian was dangerous, that you were fearful around him. There's no point in tempting fate." He leaned his face into hers and placed a soft kiss on her lips. "I don't want anything to happen to you."

Gable climbed out of bed and pulled her up with him. "So, are you ready to tackle the game room?"

They dressed and quickly put their plan into action. Once in the game room, they laughed and carried on a casual conversation about movies and books. They continued their charade for nearly an hour. At eleven o'clock Lexi went to her room and Gable went to the security office.

"How's it going, Brian?"

"Just fine, Mr. Talbot. Everything's quiet. It looks like having that reporter arrested must have made an impression on him and everyone else who heard about it."

Gable perched on the edge of the desk trying his best to appear casual. "I need to make a change in work assignments. I want to put you on days, nine in the morning until six in the evening. In fact," he glanced at his watch, "I'd like to start that new schedule right away. As you said, things have been quiet around here. Why don't you take off now so you can get some sleep and then come back for the morning shift. You will be paid for a full shift tonight, of course."

He saw the abject surprise flash across Brian's face. "But that will leave everything open tonight."

"I'm not sleepy. I'll sit in for a few hours."

"Are you sure, Mr. Talbot?" A hint of uncertainty and a level of nervousness clung to his words.

"Lexi and I were playing pool, but she gave up and went to bed. As I said, I'm not tired."

"Uh...do you mind if I ask why the change? Are you unhappy with my work?"

Gable forced a casual chuckle. "Of course not. There will be some changes happening shortly and I want to have a more efficient rotation in place before that. I'll be putting on a couple more guards, too."

Brian's reaction to the news left no confusion about Gable's head of security being rattled by this unexpected news. Would Brian be calling Prescott right away knowing full well that the three hour time difference made it a little after two o'clock in the morning on the east coast?

As soon as Brian left the house, Gable slipped out the side door and shadowed him. Rather than going back to the guard's dorm, he wandered across the lawn to the back of the yard. When he reached the trees, he made a call from his cell phone. Gable wasn't close enough to hear what was being said, but the fact that Brian made a call from an isolated location where he couldn't be overheard spoke for itself.

Gable hurried back to the security room, took his cell phone from his pocket and hit a speed dial number. A couple of seconds later he had a response on the other end. "We're set." He disconnected from the call, then phoned Ralph and the two other guards to notify them of the schedule changes.

****

"This is perfect." Lexi glanced at Gable, then read the text of the email once again before clicking the send button. "If this doesn't throw a monkey wrench in Prescott's plans, I don't know what will. It gives him what he asked for, but takes away his control of the situation."

"Exactly. My first response will be to decline his request for the party because of the adverse publicity about the skeletons. His need for control won't allow him to play a waiting game. He'll get back to you right away and have you convey to me all the reasons it has to be and he'll keep at it until I give in. That's when we hit him with our list of conditions for agreeing to his party request."

Gable checked the time. "Dolly will have breakfast ready in a couple of minutes. By the time we finish eating, we might have an answer from Prescott. Then we can hit him with the second email."

Breakfast was next on the list. Lexi went to the kitchen first rather than the two of them arriving together. Dolly and Hank were already there and, to her surprise, so was Brian. Gable joined them a few minutes later.

An uneasy feeling reverberated through Lexi's consciousness. A couple of times she caught Brian staring at her, but wasn't sure how to read his expression other than it made her nervous. She had never wanted to be finished with a meal as quickly as she did that one.

After finishing his breakfast, Gable made an announcement that caught everyone by surprise, including Lexi. "I am initiating several changes in preparation for what I anticipate being an onslaught of unwanted publicity and interruptions to the daily routine as a result of the skeletons. As I'm sure Brian has mentioned, I have changed the guards' schedules and am also putting on a couple more security guards. I've changed the locks on the Victorian mansion and instituted security measures there including a timer to turn lights on and off inside the mansion at random times. I've also made arrangements with Bud Lansing for a sheriff's deputy to make a stop here at least once a day on an arbitrary schedule of his choosing. The deputy will check with you, Brian, to make sure everything is okay, which is one of the reasons I've put you on days."

She could tell by the looks on Dolly's and Hank's faces that they were unaware of Gable changing the locks on the mansion. That one surprised her, too. For some reason he didn't want anyone to be able to get inside. Could that explain his lie to her about not changing anything on the third floor in spite of the new flat panel television? Someone would be staying there and Gable didn't want anyone to know about it? More secrets. Obviously something he didn't want to share with her, either. She didn't know whether to be unhappy or hurt that he apparently didn't trust her with the complete truth.

As anticipated, when Lexi checked her email after breakfast she found a response from Prescott about Gable's refusal to allow the party reenactment. Gable smiled when he read it, giving Lexi a knowing wink.

"He suckered into the bait. He's now playing on our terms. Let him sweat for a couple of hours, then send the next one saying I'm considering it but it doesn't look good."

"I wonder what the announcement is that he mentioned, something that will shed new light on the cold case."

"He's probably come up with a new ending for the story, one that will tie up the loose ends as a result of finding the skeletons, make him look good, and guarantee a best-seller for his book."

Lexi looked at him quizzically. "Yes, but what could that be? What kind of a new ending did he dream up that will explain everything, especially when he has to take into account that the lab can prove Winthrop is not one of the skeletons? Surely he wouldn't come up with an announcement stating Winthrop was still alive. With the varied holdings of the Hollingsworth empire extending far beyond the borders of Washington state, that would put it into federal jurisdiction and involve the FBI in a new investigation to locate Winthrop. For someone who has spent the last thirty years establishing himself as a reclusive author, that doesn't seem very logical to me."

"I'm sure we'll know soon enough. In the meantime, I'm going to start a trace on Prescott beginning with the present and working my way back to the night of the party. One way or the other, he had already made arrangements to have cash available to him when he disappeared and it had to come from the Hollingsworth fortune. I need to find when and how he was able to make the transfer of a huge amount of funds without raising any red flags on the transaction."

Gable paused as he wrinkled his brow in a moment of concentration. "I also want to call Bud Lansing and ask how they're coming with the identification of the skeletons, although it will probably take them a few days, maybe even weeks. Confirming that it's not Winthrop is one thing, but it's quite another to prove beyond a doubt that it's my father even if that's what they suspect."

The day seemed to pass quickly even though much of it became part of a waiting game between Gable and Prescott with back and forth emails setting the tone for the party reenactment that Gable wanted as much as Prescott did, but for reasons of his own. Lexi's final email to Prescott

Déjà Vu

agreed to the party, but stated that Gable's terms of agreement wouldn't be sent until the next morning. That gave Prescott all night to worry about it and further erode any control he thought he still had—a step calculated to make him careless in his actions in an attempt to regain that lost control. The ground work for Gable's revised plan had been set.

The ringing phone interrupted the work going on in Gable's office. Gable answered it and listened for a moment, then responded as if the information came as a total shock to him.

"What? You've got to be kidding, Bud! You've identified Evelyn through dental records, but the other skeleton is not Winthrop? Are you sure?"

"There's no mistake. We have Winthrop's dental records and they do not match the other skeleton. Even though Winthrop's driver's license was found with the skeleton, it's not him."

"You have verified that it's male?"

"Yes, the other skeleton is a male, six feet tall with no identifiable indications such as an old break of a leg, arm, or rib that's healed and no apparent diseases that would show up in the bones. Even without the dental records, Winthrop broke his leg in a skiing accident when he was in his twenties, so that alone would rule him out in trying to identify the other body. There's only one other person associated with this case...a male who is also missing...and that's Jack Stinson."

"Can you get his dental records?"

"Nope. We checked and the dental office burned down about ten years ago and all the old records were lost."

Gable's voice continued to convey his surprise at the startling news. "What about a DNA match?"

"So far, we don't have anything to match the skeleton to. Jack had a twin brother, Robert Stinson, who was a professional magician. He retired a couple of years ago and was reported killed in Spain in a car accident shortly after that. From the sketchy information I've been able to uncover, the body was cremated and ashes scattered at sea. Jack also had a son, a young boy at the time of the disappearances, but there isn't any information about him, either. Jack and the boy's mother had been divorced for a while. She died three years ago. It's like the son has disappeared off the face of the earth. It's possible he's living in a foreign country or he might even be dead. So, unless we can track down the son, we won't be able to do any type of DNA match to prove or disprove that the other skeleton is Jack Stinson. Right now the lab is trying to determine the cause of death on both skeletons. Is the gravesite still cordoned off?"

"Yes. I gave instructions for it to remain untouched until you released it as a crime scene and gave the all clear for us to do repairs on the foot path. Do you need to do some more work here?"

"The crime scene investigators want to do a more thorough search to see if they missed anything. I'm not sure at this point exactly what they're looking for. Possibly bullets if the bodies had been shot. Once the bodies decomposed and became only bones, any bullets embedded in the flesh or organs would have fallen through. If there are any bullets, we can try for a ballistics' match to other crimes from that time. At the very least, we'll know the type of weapon used."

"Of course. Whatever you need."

Gable disconnected from the call and turned toward Lexi. "That answers some questions. They've identified Evelyn and have confirmed the other skeleton is not Winthrop. They logically suspect it's Jack, but don't have any way of verifying it at this time." He glanced at his watch. "I want to make sure Brian has this information before his shift is over. I want Prescott to know where things stand before he gets our email in the morning. That will give him some time to revamp his plan before we throw another loop at him."

Lexi eyed him curiously. "You know, it almost seems like you're treating this as a game of some kind—a matching of wits with winner takes all as the ultimate prize."

He took her hand in his and kissed the inside of her wrist. Reveling in the warmth and emotional sensation of her touch, he brought her hand to his chest and held it there. "It is a game...of sorts."

Gable's voice took on a low, almost menacing quality. "A deadly serious game that I intend to win."

Chapter Nine

Lexi printed out the email. "Well, here it is. Prescott has agreed to your terms for allowing the party. He says he'll be here in four days, the day prior to the party, as you requested." She pointed to the last paragraph of the email. "And here's a little surprise that he has for us."

Gable took the printout and read it. "One thing for sure. We need to always be on our toes and never under estimate J.D. Prescott. After all, the mind that came up with those novels he writes is the same mind that devised the original crime, one that took thirty years and a rain storm in order to prove a crime had even been committed. So, it doesn't really surprise me that he had a list of all the original party attendees and their current locations. I'm sure he had it before he hired you to do research. All of this was carefully thought out including having a spy on my payroll."

"And according to his email, he's already extended his personal invitation to the guests for the party reenactment."

Gable's chuckle indicated part amusement and part irritation. "Looks like he's managed to salvage a bit of control in spite of our efforts." His voice turned serious. "But that's the last bit of control he'll have. Even though his inside man is working as my head of security, it won't give him the edge. In fact, it gives us the opportunity to use Brian to our advantage."

"I'm going to take that walk around the island

that was originally interrupted by the sudden appearance of the skeletons. I have something I want to run through my mind and some exercise in the fresh air will help."

Gable wrapped his arms around her and pulled her close to him. "Anything you'd like to share?"

She gave a playful pat to his rear end before pulling away from him. "You have your secrets and I have mine. Besides, I want to get it figured out first. And this time I won't have to worry about running into Brian since he's on duty."

He brushed a tender kiss across her lips. "Be careful."

Lexi returned to her room to grab a jacket, her camera, and her recorder before starting on her walk. Hank and Dolly continued to pique her interest. Even though they seemed genuinely surprised about the skeletons—Dolly seemed more horrified than surprised—they had to know something. They worked for Winthrop and were present at the party. They claimed to have been in the kitchen, but it was only their word for it without anyone else's corroborating statement.

She headed along the same path as before, until she came to the place cordoned off by the sheriff's department. She skirted the area and continued on the path. The caretaker's cottage stood to the right. She glanced back in the direction of Gable's house. Dolly was working there, but what about Hank? If she knew for certain that he wasn't in the cottage and didn't plan to be there any time soon, she would take a chance and look around inside.

Even though she didn't have anything specific in mind, she felt certain something important was inside the cottage. A hunch? Her psychic abilities poking at her? Wishful thinking? She didn't know. The only certainty being her belief that Hank and Dolly knew more than they claimed. But did they know Winthrop was still alive? That Winthrop and Prescott were one and the same person? Brian's past association had been with J.D. Prescott. Hank and Dolly's path had crossed with Winthrop Hollingsworth. Exactly who knew what about whom? Yet another puzzle piece that needed to be sorted out and put into proper perspective.

The bright sunlight warmed her mood as she continued with her walk. Her thoughts vacillated between the outward concept of turning the island into a resort and the mystery that had them ensnared in its net...a mystery as much Gable's doing as Prescott's. She quickened her pace as her thoughts turned to her immediate concern—the identification of Jack Stinson's body and how to speed it up. Ever since Gable's phone conversation with Bud Lansing about the difficulty in positively identifying the second skeleton, she had been toying with a plan—one she was sure Gable would not like, which was why she wanted to work out all the details before presenting it to him. She needed to be able to anticipate his objections and have an answer for them.

As the path rounded the far side of the island, the small sandy cove came into view. Lexi came to an abrupt halt, her attention riveted on the small boat approaching the beach. One of the men jumped out into the surf and waded ashore while the other man turned the boat around and left. Her senses jumped to full alert. She quickly hid behind some bushes so the intruder couldn't see her. Did that tabloid reporter actually think he was going to get away with sneaking on the island again?

A surge of trepidation invaded her reality and her heartbeat jumped into high gear when she realized the man was taller than the reporter and definitely much older. She couldn't see his face. But whoever he was, he seemed to know where the surveillance cameras were and how to avoid being detected.

Then one clearly defined thought popped into her mind. The intruder had to be J.D. Prescott who knew the layout because Brian told him. Where was he going? Where could he hide? Brian was on duty and couldn't do anything for a few hours yet without his absence being noticed. Prescott certainly couldn't hide out in Gable's house. With the locks having been changed on the Victorian mansion, he couldn't get inside without it being obvious that someone had broken in. Maybe Prescott had already started for the island before Brian found out about the locks? She shook her head. No, that wouldn't explain anything. All Brian had to do was call him on his cell phone and stop him from making the trip from the mainland to the island.

At least one of the other guards, if not all of them, were at the guard's temporary quarters in the building about one hundred yards behind Gable's house. That left only Hank and Dolly's cottage. She watched until the intruder was out of sight, making sure he didn't know he'd been spotted.

The urgency pounded inside her. Gable had to be told about this immediately.

As soon as the intruder was out of sight, she hurried back to the house, finally breaking into a run for the last fifty yards. Bursting through the utility room door into the kitchen, she came face to face with Dolly. She spotted Hank sitting at the kitchen table across the room.

"My goodness, Miss Caldwell. You seem all out of breath." Dolly glanced past Lexi into the garage, then returned her attention to the problem at hand. "Is everything all right?"

Lexi forced her demeanor into a calmer mode. "Yes." She extended as casual a smile as she could muster. "I've been jogging. It feels good to get the heart pounding and the blood pumping." She eased toward the hallway. "Well, I guess I'll see you later." She shot one last nervous glance in Hank's direction, then walked briskly down the hallway. Once out of sight of the kitchen, she headed for Gable's office rather than her room in the back wing.

She found the door to Gable's office locked. When she didn't receive any response to her soft knock, she took the key from her pocket and unlocked the door. Entering quickly before anyone saw her, she closed the door and locked it, then turned around.

A tight lump formed in the pit of Lexi's stomach and tried to climb up her throat. A man sat at Gable's desk, a man dressed in the same clothes the intruder at the cove wore. A moment of panic grabbed her as she reached behind for the door handle. The man raised his head. A hard jolt of shock rocked her body. She stared at the face, a face she had seen before. The same face in the computer aged photograph of Jack Stinson. The same face that had appeared in her vision before it morphed into the image of the skull. Fear replaced her shock. Her throat tried to close off, but she managed a few shaky words.

"You...you're dead!"

The man rose from the chair. "As Mark Twain said in response to an obituary printed in the newspaper, 'The reports of my death are greatly exaggerated.' As you can see, I'm very much alive."

"I believe Lexi has mistaken you for my father." The voice came from behind her, startling her already shattered nerves. She whirled around and saw Gable, a teasing grin tugging at the corners of his mouth. Her panic began to subside, but a touch of anger quickly replaced it.

She glared at Gable. "What the hell's going on here? If this isn't Jack Stinson, then who is he? Why

Déjà Vu

is he made up to look like your father and why did he need to sneak on the island?"

A hint of surprise darted across Gable's face. "Sneak on the island? You saw him arrive?"

"That's what I'm doing here. I wanted to tell you about the intruder. At first I assumed he was another reporter. Then I wondered if he was..." She stopped herself before mentioning Prescott's name in front of a stranger. She took a quick sideways look at the man behind the desk. "But I see you already know about the intruder."

Gable took her arm and escorted her to the desk. "Alexandra Caldwell, I'd like you to meet Robert Stinson, my father's twin brother, better known to the world as Santorini The Great, illusionist extraordinaire."

Lexi shook her head in an attempt to clear the fuzziness and make some sense of what he had said. "But Robert Stinson died in Spain a couple of years ago in an automobile accident. If that's who you are, then coming back from the dead is definitely a spectacular illusion."

Robert stepped out from behind the desk, extending his hand toward Lexi along with a captivating smile. "As I said, young lady, the reports of my death are greatly exaggerated."

"Uncle Robert and I have been in agreement for twenty-five years...from the time I was mature enough to get a good grasp on what had happened...that Winthrop Hollingsworth was still alive and had murdered his wife and used my father as his scapegoat. We had a long term plan that has always been behind everything either of us has done over the years. Step one was my change of identity so that Jonathon Stinson no longer existed followed by the purchase of Skull Island. Step two was Uncle Robert's retirement. Step three was his reported death. At that point, the only two people who could possibly present any type of a problem for Winthrop Hollingsworth were no longer a factor. At least that is how we intended for Winthrop to see it."

Suddenly it all made sense to her. Everything jumped into her mind in crystal clarity. She shot a quizzical look at Gable. "So your announcement about resort plans was step four? Nothing more than a ruse to draw Winthrop out into the open?"

"Yes and no. Yes in that it was step four. Certainly the probability of Winthrop having buried the bodies on the island was prominent in my mind. It made far more sense than him trying to get the bodies off the island in the days following the disappearances without any help so that no one would know he was alive. And he couldn't simply leave them in a closet somewhere as they started to decompose. If Winthrop believed there was a possibility of someone uncovering them during the construction of a resort, then he would have to do something even if it was from the safety of his new identity. And by making it known that the entire island would be dedicated to various resort functions meant no location would be safe from possible discovery. But no in that I have to admit that I like the resort plans. When this is behind us, the idea of actually building the resort is now a very real possibility."

She glanced at Robert for a moment before voicing the uppermost thought in her mind. "Would you have told me about your uncle if I hadn't seen him sneak onto the island then accidentally discovered him in your office? I assume he's the reason you changed the locks on the Victorian mansion so that no one else had access and he had a place to stay where he could remain hidden. Even your comment about lights being on random timers meant he could have lights on at night in various rooms without drawing any suspicion."

Gable's expression turned serious. "I had intended to tell you tonight when we had some time alone after dinner. Uncle Robert is going to hide out in my office until dark, then he'll go to the mansion. The third floor kitchenette has been stocked with food, there's television and computer access."

"What about my equipment?" Robert returned to Gable's desk. "Has it arrived yet?"

"The crates are warehoused at Ocean Transport's dock on the mainland. They'll be delivered this afternoon and stored in the mansion in the band room on the first floor, out of sight from anyone trying to look in the windows even though the drapes are drawn."

"Perfect. I'll unpack everything tonight and get to work on my little contribution."

Lexi looked from Robert to Gable, but neither man offered to elaborate on what had already been said. She wanted to know, but she didn't want to push Gable for more than he was ready to disclose. Her emotional attachment to Gable was intense, but she accepted that her involvement in a plan to unmask Winthrop Hollingsworth was not part of his original scheme. The majority of Gable's life...*all* of his adult life...had been spent working to bring a killer to justice and clear his father's name. Intellectually, she knew she needed to respect that and take it one step at a time, but emotionally was a more difficult situation.

And her first step would be in the morning, after she filled Gable in on the plan she had devised.

****

Lexi trailed her fingers across Gable's chest, nudging him awake. She brushed a soft kiss on his lips before sliding out of bed. He grabbed her hand and pulled her back. He held her close for a moment, then the necessity of a time frame forced them to part. She had a very busy morning ahead of her and needed to get started. The boat would pick her up at the dock in an hour and Gable had arranged a car to be waiting for her on the mainland. In spite of his initial objection, she had prevailed in convincing him of her plan to hasten the official identification of the second skeleton.

She hurried back to her room, showered and dressed, then met the boat at the dock. She found the waiting rental car at Ocean Transport's office and drove to the sheriff's lab. After introducing herself to the man responsible for identifying the second skeleton, she explained her job as a researcher...without mentioning J.D. Prescott's name or the nature of her current assignment...then got right down to business.

Lexi handed the lab technician a photograph of Jack Stinson taken the week of the disappearances. "This is a picture of the person whose skeleton you haven't been able to identify."

"Really?" The technician shot her a skeptical look. "And you know this how?"

"One step at a time." She offered a confident smile. "Verify it by the process of superimposing the skull with the photograph. I can help you with that. And when you find that it's a match, we can discuss it further."

"I'll need to notify the deputy in charge of the investigation before I can proceed with this."

"Of course. That would be Deputy Lansing?"

"Yes..." His voice trailed off as his expression changed from skeptical to questioning. He made a quick phone call, then escorted Lexi to the lab.

They worked together for several hours. She assisted him in setting up the photographic equipment and digitally matching the skull to the angle of the head in the photograph. After exactly duplicating the angle with the skull and resizing the photograph to life size, they superimposed one over the other. The technician carefully matched the width and depth of the eyes, slope of the forehead, cheekbones, definition of the jaw, shape of head, and even the shape and set of the teeth showing in the photograph…all the points of identification he could find.

Lexi nodded her head in response to the technician's obvious surprise. "Looks like a perfect match to me."

"Yes. It looks like it to me, too."

She whirled around at the sound of the voice coming from behind her and spotted Bud Lansing. "Deputy Lansing. Nice to see you again."

"Needless to say, you and I have to talk. I want to know how and why you happen to have this."

"And here…" she held out another picture toward the deputy, "is a computer aged version of that photograph showing what the subject would look like today…if he were alive. The photograph is, of course, Jack Stinson. I'm sure that doesn't come as any surprise to you. This should be sufficient proof of the skeleton's identity since there aren't any dental records or anything to match for DNA."

Bud took the picture from her and stared at the image. A slight frown wrinkled across his forehead. "Something vaguely familiar about this face." He studied it a moment longer, then stuck it in a file folder he had brought with him. "I assume I can keep this?"

"Certainly."

He stared at the screen showing the skull superimposed over the thirty-year-old photograph of Jack Stinson, then turned his attention to the technician. "Print that for me…four copies."

"And now, Lexi…" with a sweeping gesture Bud indicated the door of the lab, "shall we adjourn?"

Deputy Lansing escorted Lexi to his office and pointed toward a chair for her. "I want to hear how all of this came about. Start at the beginning." He leaned back in his chair and waited for her to collect her thoughts, the expression on his face showing a combination of keen interest and a healthy dose of skepticism.

Providing him with her carefully rehearsed story, Lexi related as much as he needed to know without revealing the underlying truth. "I was hired by J.D. Prescott to do research for a book he's writing. He wanted information about the disappearance of Winthrop and Evelyn Hollingsworth from Skull Island during a Halloween costume party thirty years ago. That entailed a trip to Skull Island because part of the information Mr. Prescott asked me to check involves the plans Gable Talbot has for building a resort on the island. As part of my research prior to arriving on the island, I procured photographs of the three missing people."

"And why did you take the time to computer age a photograph of someone presumed dead?"

"I wanted to see if it was the same face I had been seeing."

A look of surprise darted across his features. "The face you had been seeing?"

She played the part as she and Gable had devised it starting by giving the appearance of being uncomfortable with what she was about to say. And as far as discussing her psychic abilities, that wasn't far from the truth. "I...uh...I sometimes have visions. I see things."

"You mean you have psychic visions?"

"Well...yes. I don't know what else to call them. I started having a series of visions from the moment I stepped foot on the dock at Skull Island." She scrunched up the corner of her mouth as if thinking about the words she had used. "Actually it was the same vision over and over again. A face that morphed into a skull, then a mud slide and two

Déjà Vu

skeletons. A vision that became frighteningly real."

"And aging the photograph?"

"The face in my vision was not a young man. He was much older. So, after my vision of the mud and skeletons became reality, I computer aged the photographs out of curiosity. You can imagine my shock when the computer aged face of Jack Stinson turned out to be the same face from my vision. Logically, the face of Jack Stinson should have appeared as it was thirty years ago at the time of his death, not as he would look today. But for reasons I don't understand, that isn't the way it happened."

"And Gable told you about the second skeleton not being Winthrop?"

"Yes. With the other skeleton positively identified as Evelyn, that eliminated the possibility of the skeletons being associated with something else, such as a Native American burial ground Gable had mentioned as a possibility. It pretty much meant the second skeleton had to be Jack Stinson, something I'm sure you also concluded. But you would need a positive identification before you could state that as fact. Of course, this gives you a new question that needs to be answered."

"Yes. What happened to Winthrop Hollingsworth? It now seems to be a cold case that has a whole new line of investigation." He rose from his chair and came around his desk. "I certainly hope you realize what you've let yourself in for by coming forward with this."

"Excuse me?" She wrinkled her brow into a quizzical frown. "What do you mean by that?"

"Media attention. Gable has been royally pissed by the way the press has been hounding him and dredging up all the Hollingsworth stuff following his announcement of the resort plans. Then when the skeletons were discovered, that only increased the attention on Skull Island. And now with the second skeleton not being Winthrop and you providing the information that allowed us to make an identification sooner that we would have...well, you might find the next few weeks intimidating. It might calm down when you return home, assuming no one tracks down where you live. But in the interim..."

"I see what you mean." Lexi emitted an audible sigh of despair...and a calculated one. "I'll just have to handle it as best as I can. Getting to the truth is more important than any inconvenience that might come my way." The results pleased her. Just as they had planned it last night, a distraction to remove attention from Gable so he and Robert could work without being bothered. And the resulting publicity would provide an added shove to compel J.D. Prescott to make a personal appearance since he was the one who sent Lexi to the island to dig into the disappearance. It would also push him to come up with a plausible explanation about what happened to Winthrop if for no other reason than to mislead the new direction of the investigation. But perhaps he had already done that which would explain his statement that he planned to make an announcement at the party reenactment.

She glanced at her watch. Time to go. Things were beginning to come together and she was anxious to get back so she could report her success to Gable. Hopefully he had been able to discover something useful with his research into Prescott's background. Retracing her steps, she drove to the mainland dock where she returned her rental car and was ferried to the island.

Gable met her at the island dock. "I'd pull you into my arms and ravish your mouth, but I'm sure we're being watched, if not by Brian then certainly by Hank or Dolly. I'll save that little treat for later."

A sly grin tugged at the corners of her mouth. "I look forward to it." She shot him a questioning look.

Déjà Vu

"Why Hank or Dolly?"

"I'll fill you in on that later. First, tell me how everything went at the sheriff's lab?"

"Perfect. They accepted the identification and I gave Bud the story about my psychic visions, but only what we discussed. I believe he took me seriously rather than merely humoring me in order to accommodate you."

"Bud Lansing is sharp and very astute. He knows what he's doing and doesn't suffer fools lightly."

"Then why didn't you ever confide any of the truth to him rather than allow it to unfold with him in the dark about what's happening?"

"Uncle Robert and I agreed that no one would know what was going on other than the two of us. It wasn't until you were thrown into my path and started digging into things that someone else became involved."

"Kind of an unavoidable interference?"

Gable eyed her for a moment. "Yes...at first. But sharing information with you has proven to be a good decision...in more ways than one. I don't know if Uncle Robert is quite convinced yet," his teasing grin appeared, "but he will be."

"Bud said I'd probably be bombarded with media attention as soon as what I had provided the lab becomes known which, I'm guessing from his demeanor, will probably be any minute now."

"The news is already out. There have been phone calls for you." Gable drove the electric cart into the garage and plugged it in to recharge.

"How do you want me to proceed? Hold them off or schedule a news conference of sorts?"

"Neither. You'll issue an official statement. I don't want any reporters on the island, but we have to give them something so Prescott will know the official story as well as whatever Brian is telling him. I want Prescott pushed into making hasty decisions. I don't want to leave him any choice other than to keep his word and show up here the day before the party. We'll make it clear to him that if he isn't here on the island, there won't be any party."

They entered the house and proceeded directly toward Gable's office. Half way down the hall Lexi suddenly stopped walking. A sharp jolt of anxiety shot through her body. A hard lump churned in the pit of her stomach. She felt the stare boring into the back of her head. Slowly turning to look behind her, apprehension became reality when she found herself on the receiving end of Brian's cold stare.

She tried to calm her trepidation as she whispered one word. "Gable."

Brian's expression lingered only a second before being replaced with a more benign one, but it was enough of a glimpse for her to confirm the cause of the sudden shiver of fear.

Gable moved next to Lexi, his close proximity providing an immediate sense of calm and comfort. His voice projected a neutral tone that did not give away any thoughts that might have been going through his mind at that moment. "Is there a problem of some sort, Brian?"

Déjà Vu

Chapter Ten

"No, not really, Mr. Talbot." Brian leveled a penetrating look at Lexi, then returned his attention to Gable. "I need to know how you want me to handle all the phone calls for Miss Caldwell. There have been several calls from various news organizations." He tilted his head to one side and shot a questioning look at Gable, one tinged with a hint of accusation. "Is there some sort of new information that I need to be aware of? Something going on?"

"Yes, as a matter of fact there is a new development as of a few hours ago. Lexi was filling me in on the details. She just returned from aiding the sheriff's lab by providing a key piece of information that allowed them to identify the second skeleton. The lab had positively identified Evelyn Hollingsworth as one of the skeletons and eliminated any possibility of the other skeleton being Winthrop Hollingsworth. Lexi was able to positively confirm that the unidentified skeleton was the third missing person, an employee of Hollingsworth named Jack Stinson. I'm sure the media is most anxious to know what information she provided the sheriff and how she came to have it."

"I see." Brian shot another quick glance in Lexi's direction. "So, how do you want me to handle the phone calls? Will Miss Caldwell be talking to them or do I shine them on?"

Gable scrunched up the corner of his mouth for a couple of seconds as if considering Brian's

155

question. "Tell them Miss Caldwell will have a written statement first thing in the morning. She will email it to the deputy in charge of the investigation. It will be the only statement she'll be making. No one will be permitted on the island without my specific permission—no one." He paused a moment, then added. "Except the sheriff's deputies, of course."

"Yes, sir." Brian retreated toward the security office.

Lexi sucked in a calming breath as she grabbed Gable's hand and laced their fingers together. She needed the warmth and security of his touch. "You didn't see his initial expression—"

"Sh. Not here."

They continued on to the safety of Gable's office without saying anything else. As soon as they were behind the locked door, he pulled her into his arms and held her body tightly against his.

Lexi wrapped her arms around his waist. "You should have seen that look in his eyes. I knew he was behind me even before I turned around. I felt his presence...his *menacing* presence. He was staring as if trying to force information out of my head. But it was the cold look in his eyes..." She couldn't stop the shudder that rippled through her body. "It disappeared when I turned around, but not quick enough to keep me from seeing it. If I hadn't been suspicious of Brian before, this certainly would have done it."

Gable threaded his fingers through her hair as he cradled her head against his shoulder and placed a tender kiss on her forehead. "I'm so sorry you had to become involved in this, at least the part that has put you in the path of danger. But I'm so glad you've become involved in my life. It won't be much longer now. If all goes according to plan, it will be over soon. We're on the countdown to the final few days."

"About that plan...I don't want to push you or intrude where you don't want me, but there's obviously a lot more going on than you've told me about. Things like the purpose of your uncle being here, why it was necessary for everyone to think he was dead, and what kind of equipment he's setting up in the mansion."

Gable emitted a sigh of resignation as he slowly shook his head. "You've got me in an awkward position here. I want to tell you, but Uncle Robert and I have a long-standing agreement about the total secrecy of all this. I've already pushed the boundaries of our agreement by admitting my identity to you before consulting with him first. I'm not sure—"

She placed her fingertips against his lips. "It's okay. I understand." Those were her words, but not her feelings. She wanted to understand and certainly respected his integrity in keeping his word to his uncle, but she also wanted to know what was going through his mind. She was no longer an outsider looking in. She was involved and quite possibly in danger.

And what if the mess wasn't over in a couple of days? Or worse yet, what if it didn't end as Gable anticipated? Winthrop Hollingsworth had already proven himself a dangerous and elusive adversary with the money to do and buy whatever he needed whether material goods or people like Brian Cookson. If Gable's plan went awry, his life would most certainly be in danger. She refused to consider the amount of danger she would be in as well. However, she could neither ignore nor dismiss the nervous jitter that continued to push at her. Was her emotional attachment to Gable clouding her logic? Or was it her psychic energy trying to warn her of something? She didn't know.

She pulled back just enough to be able to look up

at his face. "What about you? How did your day go?"

The grin spread across his face saying how pleased he was with himself. "All in all, I'd say it went pretty well. I have a good handle on how Hollingsworth got millions of dollars into the name of J.D. Prescott. And in tracking that down, I've found another link from my little island here to Hollingsworth. What I don't know is if it also goes to Prescott."

"I don't understand." She wrinkled her brow into a half frown and half question. "After all, Hollingsworth is Prescott and Prescott is Hollingsworth. They're the same man, so wouldn't a link to one be a link to both?"

"Only if the person he's associating with knows both his true identity and his new identity. All of Brian's dealings have been with Prescott. It's very possible that he doesn't know who J.D. Prescott really is. And, conversely, it's possible that anyone who has been working for Winthrop Hollingsworth dating back over thirty years wouldn't be aware of his current alter ego."

She gave him a playful little slap on the rear end. "Stop teasing me and talking in riddles. What did you find out?"

He placed a tender kiss on her forehead. "Using the information you provided about Prescott, I was able to trace back from Prescott's current circumstance until his life intersected with Hollingsworth a year prior to Winthrop's disappearance. I don't have tangible proof yet, at least not anything that would stand up in court, but I think I know how he handled getting millions of dollars out of the Hollingsworth Empire and into the name of Prescott without raising any red flags. And also who helped him by playing a pivotal role in the transaction."

It was as if someone had switched on the light in

Déjà Vu

her head. The realization popped into her mind as clearly as if she had carefully thought it out and arrived at a logical conclusion. "Hank and Dolly. Nothing else makes any sense. They worked for Winthrop, they were on the island the night of the disappearances and they have been here ever since then. They would have been the perfect conduit to Prescott before he manipulated the circumstances that resulted in you hiring Brian and giving Prescott yet another set of eyes and ears to keep him informed about what you were doing and whether there was any danger of the skeletons being uncovered."

"Right you are. From what I've discovered, it appears that Winthrop funneled millions of dollars from the Hollingsworth Empire to a charitable organization with an account in a Swiss bank. Then the charitable organization closed its doors leaving the money in the Swiss account available to whomever had initially set it up which would, of course, have been Winthrop Hollingsworth using his already-procured new identity of J.D. Prescott. Since the Hollingsworth business enterprises did not take the charitable contribution as a tax deduction, it slipped by everyone. All of this was done a year prior to the disappearances, shortly after Winthrop's father died and he inherited everything. Apparently Winthrop's scheme to do away with his wife was a long time in the planning stage and not a last minute hasty decision or an emotionally impulsive one. It was cold, calculated and well thought out."

"How do Hank and Dolly fit into that?"

"Hank was the person listed as the financial officer for the bogus charity. The money passed through his hands on its way to Switzerland. Hank and Dolly knew he was still alive. I have no idea what kind of story Winthrop must have given him to keep him quiet after the disappearances. But, as I said, do they know his actual whereabouts and his identity as J.D. Prescott or do they think he's only Winthrop Hollingsworth still in hiding after all these years? There's still unanswered questions about Hank and Dolly. Did they understand what they were involved with at that time? Do they know now? Or are they merely dupes in Hollingsworth's elaborate scheme and cover up? Only Hank and Dolly can answer that one."

"I saw Dolly's face when she arrived on the scene and spotted the skeletons. She was genuinely shocked...and very frightened. That, put together with what you dug up, tells me she didn't know anything about the bodies being buried on the island. Maybe not even about the murders. Winthrop might have convinced them that Evelyn and Jack ran off together."

"That's a very real possibility, but doesn't negate the fact that they knew Winthrop was still alive and did not come forth with the information."

"Would it be ethical...uh, I mean...as the owner of all you survey, wouldn't you have the right to inspect their cottage?"

He slowly nodded his head. "The same thought occurred to me." A slight frown wrinkled across his brow. "On one hand it would make me feel like I was snooping into their personal life and I don't like that. But, on the other hand, you're right. I do own the cottage and have the right to inspect it for...well, for structural damage from the storm, to see if any repairs are needed. That's reaching, but I know I'm within my legal rights. It's the ethical concerns that bother me."

Stepping back from him, she made eye contact. She put as much determination into her voice as she could muster, clearly demonstrating her depth of feeling in the matter. "Your father was murdered and the man responsible has escaped any responsibility or repercussions for thirty years while continuing to live a life of luxury. You've uncovered some information that points to Hank and Dolly being involved. I think that gives you every right to pursue whatever legal avenue you find without worrying about whether it's ethical. Was it *ethical* for your father to be murdered for no reason other than supplying Hollingsworth with a scapegoat so he could murder his wife?"

She paused as she turned over a thought in her mind. Her words came out as a whisper, but clearly discernible. "And as far as I'm concerned, whatever *illegal* avenue you find is equally justified."

"I appreciate the sentiment, but I don't want to compromise anything that the prosecution can use to put Winthrop Hollingsworth behind bars. I want everything to be legal and not hand his defense team anything to work with." A hard look flashed across his face. "I don't want that bastard to walk away free and clear a second time because he can afford to buy the best attorneys available."

"I'm sorry. I certainly don't want to do anything that will cause a legal problem."

A soft chuckle escaped his throat. "That's all right. I have to admit entertaining the same notion for a moment. In fact, it's an option that probably shouldn't be totally dismissed."

"So...what's the next step?"

"Let's compose that press release you're going to email in the morning, then we'll have dinner. And after that, I think the hot tub might be a viable option to work out the kinks and stress of the day. And after that..."

A sly grin tugged at the corners of her mouth. "That's the best part."

****

Deputy Bud Lansing held up his hand to quiet the reporters gathered for the press conference.

"Alexandra Caldwell has issued a formal statement concerning her participation in the identification of Jack Stinson as the second skeleton uncovered on Skull Island and has asked me to read it. She has informed me that this will be her only statement in this matter and she will not be granting any interviews. I am also informed by Gable Talbot, owner of Skull Island, that no one will be permitted on the island without his specific permission and any attempt to illicitly gain access to the island will be treated as trespassing and will be met with criminal prosecution. And I want to add that there will not be a question and answer session following my reading of Miss Caldwell's statement."

Bud met the unhappy grumblings of the reporters with a stern expression that said he would not tolerate any disagreement or argument. He read Lexi's statement, a succinct explanation of her assignment to gather research information for J.D. Prescott for a new book and using the photograph of Jack Stinson to achieve a match with the skull. There was no further information in her statement and true to his word, Bud refused to answer any questions.

He returned to his office, slammed the door in a fit of anger, then reached for his phone. A moment later he had Gable on the line. "What the hell's going on over there? I just read this very abbreviated statement from Lexi about the identification and your edict that you'd prosecute anyone trying to get on the island. I don't know what conclusions the press has drawn from all this, but I'm not buying any of it as one big coincidence. Now that I've done your bidding, don't you think it's about time you gave me some *real* answers about what's going on?"

"Well..." Even though Gable had expected this from Bud eventually, he hadn't been prepared for it quite so soon. "You're a little ahead of me." A

Déjà Vu

nervous chuckle traveled the phone line. "I kind of thought we would probably end up having this conversation after J.D. Prescott arrived."

Bud's shock traveled the phone line back to Gable. "Prescott's coming here? Why?"

"Because I invited him. Well, actually I insisted that he pay us a visit. I imagine you've heard about the reenactment of the costume party from thirty years ago."

"Yeah, been meaning to ask you about that, too."

"It was Prescott's request. I only agreed to it if he made a personal appearance, arriving on the island at least one day prior to the party. I believe he issued a press release about having some sort of major announcement to make in conjunction with the party. My guess is that he intends to offer a solution to the mystery. Of course, it seems to me that would give away the ending for his book, but that's not my concern."

"Let me guess. Lexi's identification and statement was timed to throw a monkey wrench into his efforts."

"Very astute, Deputy Lansing. But not totally accurate."

"Suppose you fill me in."

"Suppose we continue this conversation in person rather than on the phone." Land line or cell phone, either way it was possible for someone to be listening in. And arranging a private meeting would also prolong the time before he needed to provide Bud with at least some of the truth.

"Where and when? You want me to come there or do you want to come here?"

"You come here. I want control of the surroundings so there's no possibility of an information leak. Besides, I don't want to be away from the island at this time. How about three o'clock this afternoon? I'll meet you at my dock."

"I'll be there. One more thing, before you hang up. Could you satisfy my curiosity about something else?"

A hint of caution entered Gable's voice. "And what would that be?"

"I was wondering why you always use the water taxi service from the mainland when you have a perfectly good forty-five foot pleasure yacht moored at your dock?"

"Basically, I have neither the time nor desire to be playing water taxi for everyone who comes and goes from this island."

"Don't you have someone on staff who can do that? What about Hank? Or your security people...maybe Brian or Ralph?"

"My personal boat, not a community vessel. Besides, I'm not aware of anyone on my staff who has the expertise to safely operate it."

"Makes sense. Like I said, just simple curiosity and since we were talking about truth it seemed like a good time to ask. I'll see you at three o'clock."

Gable disconnected from the call, then stared at the phone. A three o'clock meeting with Bud Lansing to discuss *the truth* had not been part of his agenda.

"Is everything all right? You look troubled."

He whirled around at the sound of Lexi's voice. "A little glitch in the plan. Bud Lansing held the press conference and read your statement."

"Isn't that what you wanted?"

"Yes, but now he's pressing me for some serious answers. I finally agreed to meet him here at three o'clock."

"Uh oh. That gives us an interesting conflict."

"What kind of conflict?"

"I just received an email from Prescott saying he's arriving today."

"Today? Damn! That probably explains the message I got from Jimmy at Ocean Transport

Déjà Vu

saying someone claims to have permission to come on the island. I'd better give Jimmy a call and see who contacted him. First Prescott didn't want to come here at all and now he's arriving a day earlier than we wanted him. Sneaky bastard. But I guess I should have been prepared for the unexpected from the likes of a master manipulator like Winthrop Hollingsworth."

"Not even lunch time yet and already it's been a weird day."

He brushed a quick kiss against her lips. "I'm afraid from here on out weird is going to be the norm. I suggest you keep that psychic radar of yours tuned in. We're going to need all the help we can get. Right now it's just you, me, and Uncle Robert against an unknown number of people and an unknown plan. Hopefully having control of the surroundings will let us control and direct whatever Prescott has in mind."

Gable had a quick phone conversation with Jimmy, then reported the latest to Lexi. "It's Prescott. He plans to be at Ocean Transport by three o'clock, assuming his flight into Seattle is on schedule, and wants to be transported to the island immediately." He stared at Lexi. "That means he'll be here at the same time as Bud and will be staying in the guest wing, same as you. I can put him at the other end of the hallway from your room, but you'd still be isolated in that wing. Maybe it would be better if you moved into my room starting tonight. I doubt that it's much of a secret about our relationship. Regardless of how careful we've tried to be, I'm sure Brian suspects and he's most likely reported his suspicions to Prescott. Maybe that's why Prescott decided to arrive a day earlier than originally set. And I'm sure Hank and Dolly suspect, too."

She wrapped her arms around his waist and

leaned her head against his shoulder. "If it wouldn't compromise any of your plans, I think I'd be more comfortable away from Prescott."

"All your sensitive research information is already securely locked away in my office safe along with your laptop computer, so any attempt to search your room won't turn up anything suspicious or critical."

"What do you want me to do? You're meeting Bud here at three o'clock and Prescott will be on the island shortly after that."

"Let's have Brian pick up Prescott at the dock. That will give him a chance to make a report in person so that Prescott will know everything we want him to know. It will also make it appear that Brian isn't on our suspect list. You'll have to greet Prescott here at the house and explain that I'm tied up with the sheriff's department with more details on the discovery of the skeletons. We'll let him worry about what the *more details* consists of. Besides, it would be an understandable thing for you to meet with Prescott. After all, he's the one who hired you and sent you here for the specific reason of gathering information. To all outside appearances, you've only done what you were hired to do and can't be held liable for the extenuating circumstances that resulted."

He leaned back enough to be able to see her face. "Are you okay with that? Meeting Prescott by yourself and keeping him occupied? Keep in mind that you'll be surrounded by people who are on his payroll in one way or another. As far as I know, Ralph doesn't have any involvement in any of this, but he also doesn't know anything that's going on beyond what's common knowledge. He'll be around, but there's no reason for him to be keeping a protective eye on you. I gave some thought to taking him into my confidence in a limited capacity, but I'm

Déjà Vu

not sure that's really a good idea. I don't want him behaving any differently toward you or anyone else, especially Brian."

She took a deep breath. "I can handle it."

He brushed a tender kiss across her lips. "I know you can."

****

Lexi couldn't decide if time flew by or crawled along. It seemed to vacillate between the two extremes until three o'clock finally arrived. Gable met Bud Lansing at the dock and took him to the Victorian mansion so they could talk without being disturbed or overheard. Did Gable plan to include his uncle in the meeting or would Robert remain safely hidden from sight? She checked her watch. Jimmy had called Brian as he left the mainland with Prescott so Brian could meet them at the dock.

Meanwhile, she had some follow up details to coordinate with the caterers for the party and needed to email last minute instructions to the party guests. All the invited guests were to gather at Ocean Transport so they could be taken to the island together rather than stragglers coming and going. The head of the catering company would make a personal inspection of the mansion's ballroom and kitchen facilities the next morning. As far as the party itself was concerned, everything moved along smoothly and on schedule.

A nervous jitter fluttered in her stomach. An uncomfortable sensation pulled at her consciousness. A vision flashed through her mind, but disappeared so quickly she didn't have a chance to recognize it. Her previous vision had turned out to be frighteningly real. The nervous jitter turned to a sick churning. She hadn't been able to discern the vision, but she had latched on to the fact that something bad was going to happen. If only she knew what and when. The only thing she felt for certain was a sense of danger for someone, but she didn't know who.

After checking with the caterer and sending the emails, she returned to her room and moved her personal belongings before Prescott arrived. She watched from Gable's bedroom window as Brian drove the electric cart to the dock.

Sucking in a deep breath, holding it and slowly exhaling did not do anything to calm her anxiety. Another fifteen minutes or so and she would be face to face with J.D. Prescott. Somehow she had to maintain her composure and project a persona that said there wasn't anything wrong.

Then, sooner than she wanted, she saw Brian returning with a passenger in the cart...a passenger whose face she couldn't see. The cart disappeared into the garage. She steadied her nerves, then headed for the kitchen to greet the guest. She arrived just in time to see Brian's back as he escorted the new arrival toward the guest wing in the back.

She paused in the kitchen to get a drink of water. As she raised the glass to her mouth, the vision flashed through her mind again only this time it lingered long enough for her to get a fleeting glance at it. A man...a faceless man...pointing a hand gun and firing point blank range at someone standing in the shadows. A cold chill jolted through her body. With a shaking hand, she set the glass of water on the counter. The sick churning tried to work its way up her throat. It took all her will power to keep her panic in check.

The man had fired the gun at Gable!

She tried to force the vision to return. There had to be something there to help her identify the gunman even without any facial features. His clothes. His hair. His size. The setting. Any background details that would tell her where it would take place. There had to be something—

Déjà Vu

"Miss Caldwell."

Brian's voice shattered the silence, cutting through her icy panic. She looked around and saw him standing at the kitchen door with another man. A moment of total confusion assaulted her senses. Was this supposed to be J.D. Prescott? Something was drastically wrong. Winthrop Hollingsworth would be sixty-five years old. The man with Brian looked about fifty and stood a couple of inches shorter than Winthrop's known height of six feet. Was the entire premise she and Gable had put together about Prescott really being the long missing Winthrop Hollingsworth nothing more than wishful thinking without any basis in fact?

The man stuck out his hand and extended a polite smile. "It's nice to be able to greet you in person, Miss Caldwell. May I call you Alexandra?"

She rallied her senses, forcing the confusion from her mind while trying to present a calm and casual outer appearance. "Please, call me Lexi. It's certainly a pleasure to meet you, Mr. Prescott. It's nice to finally put a face and voice to all those emails we've exchanged." The moment she grasped his hand, she knew he was lying. Whoever he was, he definitely was not J.D. Prescott.

"I'll leave you with Miss Caldwell. If you need anything, just give me a shout."

"Thank you, Brian. I'll be just fine." As soon as Brian left for the security office, the man claiming to be J.D. Prescott turned his attention to Lexi. "We have some work details to handle, but first I'd like to meet Mr. Talbot. I rather thought he would be the one picking me up at the dock. Is he on the island?"

"Yes, he's here. However, he's tied up in a meeting with the deputy in charge of the investigation of the skeletons."

"Oh? Is there some new information?"

"I don't know. Deputy Lansing called a few

hours ago and arranged to meet with Gable this afternoon. I don't know what he wanted to discuss. I don't think Gable knew, either." She saw it in his eyes, a look that said he wasn't sure how to respond to what she had said but knew he had to say and do something.

A slight frown wrinkled across his forehead. "I see. Well, shall we get down to business? I want to go over the party details with you."

"Gable has graciously set aside the den for us to use as a temporary working area. I have the party information laid out on the table. I assumed that would be first on your list since the big event is only two days away. I do know that Gable wants to discuss your big announcement. In fact, I believe he's preparing an announcement of his own."

"And just what does Gable Talbot intend to announce?" A hint of an edge clung to his words.

"I think I can answer that one." Gable strode confidently into the room, grabbing their immediate attention.

"Gable...your meeting with Deputy Lansing is over already?"

"Just concluded."

"I'd like you to meet J.D. Prescott. Mr. Prescott, this is our host, Gable Talbot."

The two men shook hands. "Mr. Prescott. A pleasure."

Lexi noted the quick flicker of curiosity tinged with a touch of surprise that darted through Gable's eyes.

Gable extended his most charming smile. "You're much younger than I thought you would be. You must have written your first novel when you were still a teenager. That's very impressive."

"It seems like I've been writing all my life." A nervous chuckle followed Prescott's words, one that seemed to Lexi to be forced and as out of place as his non-answer type of answer. Something was definitely wrong...something in addition to the too young and too short man claiming to be J.D. Prescott. She needed some time alone with Gable to compare notes as soon as possible.

"Lexi, why don't you go over your party preparations with Mr. Prescott while I take care of a few things in my office, then I'll join you."

She shot Gable a curious look. This wasn't part of their initial plan. "Sure thing. We can start with the guest list. I've requested that each guest include a description of their costume along with their RSVP."

A quick glance in Gable's direction as he left the den told her more than his parting comment did. His manner appeared casual, but she detected the tension in his body. He had obviously found this man claiming to be J.D. Prescott as suspicious as she did.

****

Gable proceeded to the security office. "Thanks, Brian, for picking up Prescott at the dock. Bud Lansing had been insistent about meeting with me this afternoon so I thought I'd better humor him."

"Anything new on the investigation?"

"Nothing yet. A thirty-year-old murder is definitely a cold case. We know Evelyn Hollingsworth was murdered and now we know Jack Stinson was the other skeleton, a second murder victim buried in the same grave presumably by the same person. That leaves us with the tantalizing and unanswered question of what happened to Winthrop Hollingsworth. He isn't accounted for and it's a given fact that Evelyn and Jack didn't bury themselves." Gable tilted his head to one side and leveled a steady look in Brian's direction. He studied the way Brian's gaze nervously darted around the room, landing everywhere except on Gable. "Any theories?"

171

"Well...now that you mention it, I have been giving the matter some thought ever since they said the second skeleton wasn't Winthrop."

"Let's hear what you came up with."

Brian shifted his weight in his chair, his demeanor appearing uncomfortable...and increasingly nervous.

"Uh...yes...well, it seems obvious that Winthrop must have had a hand in it."

"And?"

"And, what?"

"And what happened to Winthrop? And why would he have killed his wife and this other man who was only an employee?" Gable paid close attention to Brian's body language.

"Yeah...well, maybe he...uh...I mean he killed them and then someone else killed him."

"Really?" No doubt about it. Brian's value to Prescott was muscle, intimidation and the collection of information. It wasn't subtleness, guile, thinking on his feet, or his ability to convincingly play a part. "That's an interesting theory. Do you have any notions about who would have killed Winthrop...or why? And what happened to Winthrop's body since it's never been found?"

"Uh...maybe it was...what about that brother of Stinson's...the one who..." A scowl crossed Brian's face followed by a clenching of his jaw. "How the hell would I know? It was just a thought. Forget it."

Gable quickly changed the subject. "I want you to keep your eyes glued to those security cameras. Between Lexi's announcement this morning and the reclusive J.D. Prescott arriving on the island this afternoon, I'm expecting a flurry of trespassing attempts. I don't want anyone on this island who hasn't been cleared by me."

"Yes, sir, Mr. Talbot."

The next stop for Gable was Prescott's room in

the guest wing. With Lexi keeping Prescott occupied in the den and Brian relegated to the security office, it was the perfect time for Gable to look through Prescott's belongings. They had a little over forty-eight hours to bring all the pieces together. Then it would be the evening of the costume party reenactment. Everything had to be in place prior to the party.

It was risky and the timing critical.

Everything...twenty-five years of dedication and several years of concentrated effort all came down to the night of the party. All or nothing. And Gable Talbot refused to settle for nothing as the outcome of his efforts. He didn't know the true identity of the man claiming to be J.D. Prescott, but he did know that it definitely was not Winthrop Hollingsworth. So, just who was this imposter?

And exactly where was Winthrop Hollingsworth?

Chapter Eleven

"This way, Mr. Prescott." Brian pointed to the security camera as he led the sixty-five-year-old man on a circuitous route from the cove through the trees toward the house. "Ralph is having dinner right now. We've got a ten minute window without anyone monitoring the cameras, but we've got to hurry."

"How is my stand-in handling the situation? Does anyone suspect he's an imposter?"

"Not that I'm aware of. Miss Caldwell greeted him and they went to the den to go over the party details. Mr. Talbot didn't show any indication of being concerned." Brian paused for a moment, as if not sure whether to say any more. He continued hesitantly. "He did question me about any theories I might have on what happened to Winthrop Hollingsworth."

Prescott stopped walking and eyed Brian with a sharp stare. "And what did you tell him?"

"Well...uh, I said what you told me to. That maybe it was Hollingsworth who killed them and he was probably killed by the brother. Mr. Talbot didn't say much other than for me to keep a sharp eye on the monitors because he anticipated several attempts by people trying to sneak on the island." Brian glanced at his watch. "We need to hurry, Mr. Prescott."

"What's that?" J.D. Prescott pointed toward the Victorian mansion. "Why are there lights on inside? Is someone working on party preparations?"

"Not that I'm aware of. Mr. Talbot said he

installed added security at the mansion and had lights on timers to come on and go off in various rooms at random times. Starting tomorrow there will be activity in the mansion. The caterer will be inspecting the kitchen facilities and Mr. Talbot will have people setting up for the party."

Prescott continued to stare at the mansion for several seconds before returning his attention to Brian. "You're sure no one is staying in the mansion?"

"Everyone on the island is accounted for. You are the only unknown person here. There is one more thing, though. I can't prove it, but I think Talbot and the Caldwell woman are sleeping together. They've been cautious, but not careful enough."

"An affair? Well, that was quick work on someone's part. Do you know which one of them initiated it?"

"No, sir. As I said, I don't have any proof. It's not like I've seen them with their tongues down each other's throats or one of them sneaking out of the other one's bedroom before sunrise."

"Well, that's an interesting bit of information for me to file away."

"I have to apologize for the size of my quarters, but there's nowhere else for you to stay where you'll be out of sight."

"Yes, I understand."

Brian led Prescott to the building behind Gable's house being used as temporary housing for the security guards, each guard having a bedroom with sitting alcove and private bath. As soon as he had Prescott settled in, he returned to the security office inside Gable's house.

Ralph looked up as Brian entered. "What are you doing here? Is there a problem of some kind?"

"No...just checking in to make sure everything

was quiet. Mr. Talbot was concerned that all the publicity in the last day or two would result in increased attempts by the media to get on the island."

"Everything is quiet here. Mr. Talbot, Miss Caldwell, and that author fellow have been in the den since dinner. I believe Mr. Talbot said they were working on plans for the costume party." Ralph took a large swallow from his coffee mug followed by a grimace. "Damn...I hate cold coffee."

Ralph dumped the remaining coffee from his mug and refilled it with fresh from the coffee pot. Settling back in his chair, he took a sip of the hot coffee then continued. "From what I've heard, the party sounds like it's going to be quite an elaborate function."

"It's supposed to duplicate the original party from thirty years ago, back when the power brokers of the time all gathered here for social occasions. It must have really been something back in those days. Have you ever taken a really good look inside the mansion? High dollar all the way."

Brian stayed a couple of minutes longer until he was convinced Ralph didn't suspect anything, then headed toward the den so he could get a handle on what was going on with the imposter and report back to Prescott.

He stuck his head in the door. "Everything all right in here, Mr. Talbot?"

Gable looked up at the intrusion. "Yes...everything is fine. We're nailing down the details for the costume party." He straightened and took a couple of steps toward the door. "The caterer will be here at ten o'clock in the morning to check the kitchen and serving facilities in the mansion. He'll be bringing a three man work crew with him to start setting up. That should already be noted on your log for tomorrow."

Déjà Vu

"Yes, sir. Will there be anything else tonight?"

"Not a thing, Brian. Thank you."

Gable watched as Brian left the den, then turned his attention back to Lexi and the imposter. He caught the fleeting look of curiosity that darted across her face. "Sorry about the interruption. Now, where were we?"

They worked for two more hours, then decided to call it a night. Gable suggested a drink before retiring for the evening. The three of them went to the bar. Gable kept the conversation to superficial topics, aware that either Hank or Dolly or Brian could easily be listening...possibly all three of them.

"Well, Mr. Prescott. You communicated to Lexi that you intended to make a special announcement at the party. Exactly what is it you plan to say?"

"I want it to be a surprise. I don't want anyone getting wind of it before I have my say." He eyed Gable with a hint of caution. "Do you have a problem with that?"

"Well, frankly...I do. This is my private residence. The entire island is private property. If you intend to make some sort of formal announcement that will have an adverse impact on me or my property, I have the right to know what it is otherwise I might refuse to allow it."

The imposter visibly bristled at Gable's harsh words. "You can't keep me from making a statement to the press."

"You're right, but I can prevent you from doing it here and creating more of a three ring circus than already exists. In other words, Mr. Prescott...I can kick your ass off my island any time I choose without danger of repercussions."

A moment of panic darted through the imposter's eyes as he visibly tried to gather his composure and smooth over what Gable had purposely turned into an awkward confrontation.

177

Gable could tell from Lexi's expression that she wasn't sure what he was up to, but was enjoying his manipulation of the situation.

A forced chuckle escaped the imposter's throat as he awkwardly shifted his position on the bar stool. "Really now, Mr. Talbot...uh, Gable...I don't want to create a problematic situation here. I simply thought we could do each other some good. I've uncovered the solution to what really happened here thirty years ago. I can use it to promote my book and you could use the resulting publicity to promote your resort."

"And you thought sensationalizing a multiple murder would be the best way of promoting a family resort?"

"Sensationalizing a multiple murder? That's certainly not my intention. I plan to offer my help to the authorities in the form of a solution to the murders so they can finally close the case."

Gable tilted his head as he raised his eyebrows in a questioning manner. "And just what would that solution be?"

"Look, let's compromise on this. I'll provide you with a written copy of my statement prior to the party. How about that? You'll know what I'm going to say even before the authorities do."

There was no mistaking the stress level in the imposter's voice. He was doing a much better job of playing his part than Brian, but he had not been coached on all the possibilities of where the conversation could go and how to handle them. "Let me think about that. I'll give you my decision at breakfast in the morning."

"Well, that seems fair. And maybe you will be good enough to let me know what it is you plan to announce?"

"And what makes you think I'm planning to make an announcement?"

Déjà Vu

"Well...it seems like the logical thing for you to do since I'm making a statement to the press. I want to make sure we aren't conflicting each other."

Lexi paid close attention to the back and forth verbal sparring between Gable and the man claiming to be J.D. Prescott. She could tell Gable was baiting him, but she didn't know exactly why. Whatever the reason, Gable must have been satisfied with the results because he let it drop and turned the conversation to routine matters.

"Tell me, Mr. Prescott..."

"Yes, Lexi? What is it?"

"We've gone over the costume list of the invited guests and all those attending have agreed to wear the same type of costume they wore thirty years ago. Gable thought it would be interesting if he and I wore the same costumes that Winthrop and Evelyn wore that night. What costume do you plan to wear?"

Another forced chuckle greeted her question, although this one didn't seem as uncomfortable. "I was thinking about wearing a Stephen King mask, but decided against it. I finally settled on a cowboy outfit."

She jerked to attention. *A cowboy? With gun belt, holsters...and loaded six-shooters?* "That should be fun. The traditional cowboy hat, chaps, vest, and boots? Are you going to be the good cowboy sheriff or the bad cowboy bank robber?"

"I'm prepared for either choice, but I haven't made the decision yet." The imposter glanced at his watch. "I've had a long day and it's three hours later on the East Coast where I started out this morning. So, if you'll both excuse me, I think I'll turn in for the night."

He eased off the bar stool and extended his hand toward Gable. "Thank you for your hospitality." Then he turned his attention toward Lexi. "It was a pleasure to finally meet you. I want to go over your research information in the morning so I can put the finishing touches to my statement for the press."

"Of course, Mr. Prescott. Good night." She watched as the imposter left the bar to return to his guest room.

As soon as he was out of sight, she turned to Gable. "Did you catch the bit about his costume? A cowboy means a gun belt—"

"Sh." He placed his fingers against her lips. "Later."

Gable and Lexi gathered the paperwork from their meeting with the Prescott imposter and locked it in the office, then headed for his bedroom suite. Once behind closed doors, he pulled her into his arms and placed a tender kiss on her lips.

"Yes, I heard the cowboy bit. I'll have to make sure he doesn't have any live ammunition in those six-shooters...just in case. I also noticed that the man claiming to be Prescott was much too young. I took the liberty of searching his room while you had him occupied in the den and after I made sure Brian was staying in the security office."

She waited for him to continue. When he didn't say anything else she gave him an affectionate swat on the rear end. "And?"

A teasing grin tugged at the corners of his mouth. "Oh...you mean you want to know what I found?"

"Of course I do!"

A soft laugh accompanied the quick kiss he brushed against her lips. "According to the identification he had tucked away in his suitcase, his name is Hal Bentley and he's an actor."

"An actor? I never heard of him and I didn't recognize his face."

"Even though he's fifty-one years old, he's only a struggling actor whose experience is limited to Off-Broadway productions. Prescott chose carefully in

Déjà Vu

picking someone who needed the money, could play a part, and whose face and name wouldn't be known to either you or me. After giving it some thought, I have to admit it was a logical and necessary move for Prescott to make. Most of the people attending the party knew Winthrop and even with the passing of thirty years, they would most likely be able to recognize him. He couldn't take that chance. So, when I pressured him to be here, he had to provide an imposter in his place. And to further distance himself from the about-to-be-public persona of J.D. Prescott, he chose a mature yet younger man to play the part."

"But Winthrop has to show up. He can't afford not to have his hand in what's happening here. His very life literally depends on him not being unmasked and that includes someone unmasking his imposter. It's an area where he can make an attempt at maintaining control."

"I know. In fact, I wouldn't be overly shocked to find that Prescott is already on the island and Brian has him hidden away somewhere. I could do a surprise inspection of his living quarters, but not without tipping our hand. And there's still Hank and Dolly as part of the equation, too. And the big unanswered question…does Brian know Prescott is really Winthrop Hollingsworth and do Hank and Dolly know Winthrop's new identity as J.D. Prescott?"

"How do we go about proving any of what we suspect?"

Gable took a steadying breath, hoping it would calm his nerves. He felt sure Lexi wasn't going to be happy with what he had to say next, but the plan he and Uncle Robert had meticulously worked out was already in play. It was their best chance at being able to unmask the real Winthrop Hollingsworth and make him pay for his crimes.

He threaded his fingers through the silky strands of her hair and cradled her head against his shoulder. When all of this was over...when the future was once again a clean slate to be filled in with all the possibilities, a future that he hoped would include Lexi, but for now...

"First thing in the morning I'll be making a statement to the press. I'm going to admit my true identity and say that I've given a DNA sample to the sheriff's department to confirm my relationship to the second skeleton. Then I'm going to accuse Winthrop Hollingsworth of murdering both my father and Evelyn and claim he has been living under a new identity for all these years. My statement will say that I intend to expose him and prove he's a cold blooded killer, something that will happen at the recreation of the party where the original crime was committed."

The alarm covered her face. "But that puts you in extreme danger."

He tried to force a casual smile and manner. "As they say...no pain, no gain."

An angry scowl distorted Lexi's features. "Stop talking like an idiot. You can't put yourself in that kind of danger. If anything happens to you, the entire plan goes down the drain. All you've worked for—"

"Nothing is going to happen to me." He tightened his hold on her, needing the closeness and comfort.

"I promise you, Lexi. Everything is going to be okay. I can't divulge all the details. Uncle Robert and I—"

"I know. You've given your word and I respect that. But it doesn't mean I'm happy about the situation."

"I know." He trusted her, absolutely and completely. That wasn't the problem. More than

Déjà Vu

anything he wanted to be able to share everything with her. But his promise...his sacred word that had been in play for years...could not be compromised without Robert's permission. And his uncle had been reluctant to allow him to share the most intimate and carefully guarded details of their plan.

"If you get yourself hurt, if anything happens to you I'll..." her voice trailed off. She couldn't bring herself to finish the sentence. If anything happened to him she knew part of her would die.

He continued to speak, but his words did not comfort her even though his voice was soothing. "If stepping forward and giving my true identity doesn't stir up a hornet's nest, then I don't know what will. That's going to force Prescott into doing something for sure. He can't afford to have Jack Stinson's son running around making accusations. Whatever Prescott planned to announce at the party will be drastically overshadowed when the press hears what I have to say."

Skepticism surrounded her words. "Don't you think that sounds just a tad theatrical?"

"Hollingsworth turned himself into J.D. Prescott and has surrounded his entire life with the theatrical ranging from becoming the author of horror novels to the reclusive persona he created. Even his insistence on recreating the party from the night of the disappearances reeks of the theatrical. The one thing he can't allow is for Jack Stinson's son to present surprising new information in the case."

Gable placed a tender kiss on her cheek. "Whatever claims the imposter has been instructed to make about the case won't be worth anything. Not only will Prescott need to alter his plan, he'll need to do it on the fly while remaining in hiding on Skull Island which will drastically curtail his movements. And if he's as clever as I think he is, he'll assume any and all cell phone and computer communication to and from this island can be monitored and even terminated if I choose. That leaves him with a maximum of four cohorts if we include his hired actor who probably thinks he's nothing more than a player in one of J.D. Prescott's works of fiction and has no knowledge of what's really going on."

"What about Deputy Lansing? How is he going to take this news? He probably won't be too pleased to learn who you really are and how you've been manipulating things right under his nose."

"I apprised Bud of that when we met this afternoon. You're right. He was not pleased that I had kept things from him, but understands why."

"Did you tell him everything? Introduce him to your uncle Robert?"

"No. Uncle Robert is my secret weapon. However, I do need to bring Bud up to date on another development. I didn't know about Prescott's imposter until after my meeting with Bud. I want him to run a background check on Hal Bentley to confirm he's nothing more than an out-of-work actor hired by Prescott."

"Did you tell Bud about Prescott and Winthrop Hollingsworth being one and the same person?"

"No. I don't have any proof yet and won't until he comes out of hiding. And that, if all goes according to plan, should be at the party."

Lexi wrapped her arms around his waist as she slowly shook her head. "I sure hope you know what you're doing."

****

Deputy Bud Lansing looked out at the stunned expressions of the assembled members of the media. "That concludes Mr. Talbot's statement. Thank you ladies and gentlemen."

"A question Deputy Lansing, if you please."

Bud leveled a dubious stare at the tabloid reporter Gable had charged with trespassing. "I

Déjà Vu

thought I made it clear that I'm not holding a press conference. I'm merely presenting Mr. Talbot's statement and confirming that we have received the DNA sample from him and are processing it."

"Perhaps I misspoke." Tom Jackson's lip curled in a sneer. A self-satisfied smirk covered his face. "I don't have a question, I have a comment. I believe it's blatantly obvious that the great Gable Talbot...or whatever his name is this week...is using the sheriff's office to promote his personal agenda and you seem to be happily ensconced in his back pocket. Just how much money is he paying you to do his bidding?"

Bud's expression turned to an angry glare. His voice took on a low, menacing quality that left no doubt about the seriousness of the warning. "That sounds like a question to me and one dangerously close to slander. I suggest you use more caution in choosing your words in the future. One more comment like that and I will arrest you."

With that, Bud left the lobby and went to his office. He slammed down the typed copy of Gable's statement, then turned to face Gable seated across the desk. His anger surrounded every word. "I assume you heard that little bastard's comment?"

"Yeah. One of these days he's going to say the wrong thing to the wrong person. That big mouth and obnoxious manner of his will land him in the hospital. I know I've sure been tempted to pop him a couple of times."

"Well, I can't say that I disagree with what he said. It sure looks that way. All of this going on right under my nose. Skeletons uncovered and you don't say a word about anything, acting like it was as much of a surprise to you as it was to everyone else. Sending Lexi here with that photograph and still staying in the background and not filling me in on the truth." He leveled an angry scowl at Gable. "I gotta ask...what else is there that you haven't told me? What other surprises do you have in store for me that will end up making me look like either an inept fool or your puppet?"

Gable paused as he contemplated Bud's question. "Nothing that I can talk about right now. I'll fill you in as soon as I can."

"You do know that there are laws against withholding evidence and interfering with the investigation of a criminal case, don't you?"

"Evidence? I don't have any evidence, only my suspicions. I *know* what happened, who's responsible, and where he's been all these years. What I don't have is anything tangible that bears a resemblance to proof...yet."

"You're playing a dangerous game, Gable. I hope it doesn't blow up in your face with you caught in your own manipulations."

"Sort of hoist with my own petard?" A sigh of resignation passed through Gable's lips. "I know, Bud. All I can do is ask for your indulgence a little while longer. That and one more favor."

"You're wanting more than I've already acquiesced to?" The incredulity in Bud's voice rang loud and clear. "What is it this time? You want my arm and leg? Maybe want me to throw in one of my kidneys for good measure?"

Gable couldn't stop his laugh. "No, nothing that dramatic. At least not yet." His manner turned serious again. "I want you to run the name Hal Bentley, age fifty-one, New York City. A mostly out-of-work actor whose current role is impersonating reclusive author J.D. Prescott. As of late yesterday afternoon he's temporarily staying in one of the guest rooms at my house. I want to know if out-of-work actor is true and all there is to it or if there's more."

"Are you sure you know what you're doing?

Déjà Vu

Innocent people could get hurt. Or worse yet…killed. I can't protect someone when I don't know who I'm protecting or what I'm protecting them from." Bud shook his head in resignation. "At least you have a security staff on the island. Brian's been in the business for quite a while and ought to know what he's doing."

Gable visibly winced at the deputy's mention of Brian. Far from help, Brian was yet another problem to be dealt with. "Just a couple of days, Bud. By tomorrow night at the party everything will be out in the open."

"Hal Bentley." Bud wrote the name on a piece of paper along with the other information Gable had given him. "I'll see what I can find."

"Thanks, Bud. I appreciate your indulgence and I promise you'll be the first to know what's going on."

Leaving the sheriff's station by the back door to avoid being spotted by the reporters, Gable returned to the island. He arrived just in time to meet Lexi and the caterer in the den at his house. He quickly took charge of the situation.

"Your work crew's unloading at the dock. I'll have Hank and one of my security guards give them a hand in transporting everything to the mansion. After inspecting the facilities, I imagine you'll have a few items to add to the list. Have whatever you need taken to the mainland dock at Ocean Transport and I'll have it brought over."

Gable made a quick call to Hank giving him instructions, then he escorted Lexi and the caterer to the mansion. After the caterer inspected the kitchen facilities, Gable walked him through all the areas being used for the party which consisted of everything on the main floor…all except one small room that connected to the ballroom. A windowless room with locked doors.

"I must say, Mr. Talbot, this far exceeds my

expectations. You've certainly done a marvelous job of bringing the kitchen facilities up to date and then some. I hadn't anticipated a large gourmet kitchen. I don't foresee any problems at all. Plenty of work room in the kitchen and we can use the informal dining area for our staging so the servers won't have any need to come into the kitchen to deposit dirty glasses and pick up filled trays. That will drastically cut down the congestion and clogged traffic patterns and let everything move much more smoothly."

"Lexi has shown me the menu for the party. Everything seems to be in order. I realize this is a large function and it was all heaped on you at the last minute without your usual lead time for preparation. I appreciate your cooperation and professional attitude. I'll certainly keep it in mind with regard to the resort's needs."

Leaving the caterer and his crew to set up for the party, Lexi and Gable returned to his house. They grabbed some lunch, then secreted themselves in the office.

A hard jolt of fear hit Lexi. Her body stiffened as the disturbing image flashed through her mind again. A shadowy figure with a gun, someone shooting at Gable. Hard shivers of foreboding jittered through her body. She slipped her arms around his waist seeking some kind of comfort and reassurance.

His expression quickly changed from one of pleasure at her perceived intimate advance to one of concern. He wrapped his arms around her and held her close. "You're trembling. What's wrong?"

"A vision...I've had another vision. A man—a faceless man firing a hand gun at point blank range directly at—" A sob caught in her throat. "Directly at you. That's all I saw. No background details to tell me where, nothing to indicate when, but it was enough. I'm frightened for you, Gable...for your safety. You know Brian is working for Prescott, knows the island and has access to most everything. He's also a trained expert with firearms. You know the man claiming to be Prescott is someone else who may even be a dangerous assassin. And you also know Hank and Dolly are involved with Winthrop Hollingsworth and probably know he's very much alive. They may even know his current whereabouts and new name. By revealing your true identity to everyone you've purposely set yourself up as a target."

He ran his fingers through her hair and rested his cheek against her head. His words came out soft and tender. "I'm going to be just fine...regardless of what your psychic abilities are telling you."

"My vision was right about the skeletons and about your father's face. This new vision is just as strong. I can't ignore it."

"All I can do is ask you to trust me."

"But you don't trust me. You've purposely left me out in the cold about what you and Robert are doing, about what's really going to happen tomorrow night at the party."

He took a calming breath. "I don't like that part of it, either. As I said before, I don't like keeping secrets from you. Please believe me. It doesn't have anything to do with trusting you. Uncle Robert and I made a pact long ago that neither of us has broken. I gave him my word of honor."

"But my vision—"

Gable brought his mouth down on hers, partly to satisfy his desire to kiss her and partly to stop her words. Not being able to fully confide in her weighed heavily on his shoulders, but he had given his word and was honor bound to stand by it.

His kiss deepened. He had never felt more at one with any other woman. After tomorrow night everything would be over, the past would be resolved, and he would be free to share his feelings with her...assuming he could clearly define those feelings. For now, however, other things had to take precedence.

And that included making sure of Lexi's safety.

Even though Gable broke the kiss, he did not relinquish his hold on her. He felt torn in two directions. He didn't want her to leave. Not now. Not tomorrow. Not ever? But his practical and logical side confirmed what he needed to do. He forced out the words.

"I think it would be a good idea if you left the island until this is over. If there is someone with a gun who's going to try and take a shot at me during the party, I don't want any possibility that you might end up in the line of fire."

She jerked back from his embrace, shock covering her face. "But I can't leave! I'm playing the part of Evelyn Hollingsworth at the costume party."

He grasped her shoulders and fixed her with a hard stare. His voice conveyed the depth of his resolve and concern. "And Evelyn ended up dead. I won't allow that to be even a remote possibility with you. You'll be safer away from the island."

A hard look of determination settled over her features. "No. Unless you're prepared to hog-tie me and physically throw me on a boat against my will, I'm not leaving. Besides, I'll be much safer here. Prescott certainly knows I'm involved. After all, he's the one who hired me and sent me here to do research. Everyone knows I'm the one who supplied the photograph to the lab for the initial identification of Jack Stinson. Leaving the island won't make me safe. In fact, I'm probably safer here where access is limited than I would be on the mainland."

He pulled her into his arms again.

He didn't like it, but had to admit she was right

about probably being safer on the island. He placed a tender kiss on her lips before reluctantly turning loose of her. An audible sigh of resignation escaped into the air. "You're very persuasive." *Too persuasive. But if anything happens to you, I won't be able to live with it.* "There are a few things we can discuss, things we need to accomplish during the party."

Chapter Twelve

The Victorian mansion shone like a diamond with brilliance reflected from every facet, ablaze with lights for the glittering affair. Music filtered from the ballroom out to the large terrace and through the ground floor. Champagne flowed freely along with a plentiful supply of various hors d'oeuvres.

Gable and Lexi were costumed as the same characters Winthrop had chosen for himself and Evelyn thirty years ago—Henry VIII and Anne Boleyn. It had been an apt choice for Winthrop to have made...the king of all he surveyed and the wife who ended up dead. Gable greeted the arriving guests at the mansion's front door. Per his instructions, all the invited guests had gathered at the Ocean Transport dock and were ferried to the island in one large group after presenting their invitations and identification, then being checked off the list.

The festivities quickly got underway. Even though the reason for the costume party was a serious one, the invited guests from years gone by seemed to be enjoying themselves. Old friends catching up and reminiscing about past parties at the mansion. Others renewing past acquaintances. To all outward appearances it was yet another of the lavish affairs thrown at the Hollingsworth mansion in years gone by.

Lexi introduced each of the guests to the Prescott imposter, making sure everyone knew J.D.

Prescott would be making a major announcement later that evening. She kept a watchful eye on the six-guns that were part of his cowboy costume, trying to determine if they were merely props or functional weapons loaded with real bullets. Bud's check on Hal Bentley hadn't revealed anything other than an out-of-work, struggling actor, but caution remained the order of the day.

Anxiety continued to poke at Lexi's senses, a low level ripple that refused to go away. She stole a quick glance at Gable. To all outward appearances he represented the epitome of calm, cool, and collected as he charmed his way through the guests. But she saw through that to the tension beneath the surface.

Gable stopped the music, then called for everyone's attention. "Ladies and gentlemen...welcome to Skull Island. As you are all aware, at the request of best-selling author J.D. Prescott, we're recreating the costume party from the night Winthrop and Evelyn Hollingsworth disappeared, a party attended by many of you." He made an elaborate gesture toward the Prescott imposter who acknowledged the announcement with a bow to the guests.

"As you may know if you've been following the media coverage of the recent discovery of two skeletons on the island, Mr. Prescott has been researching what happened here years ago in conjunction with his new book and plans to make a statement later this evening about the case and this unexpected turn of events. I have a statement of my own that I will be making after that. But for now—" he restarted the music, "let the party begin."

Gable put on the mask that covered most of his face, then held out his hand toward Lexi. She donned her mask before taking his hand. They were the first ones on the dance floor. Within a couple of minutes the other couples filled the dance floor just as it had been that night thirty years ago.

Gable held Lexi close as he whispered in her ear. "Are you ready?"

The nervous tension carried into her voice in spite of her attempt to suppress it. "As ready as I'll ever be."

He danced her toward the open French doors that led to the terrace, exiting through one set of doors so they were out of sight from everyone else. Then a moment later Anne Boleyn and Henry VIII danced back into the ballroom through another set of French doors. Large outdoor heaters had been placed around the terrace making it comfortable enough for guests to be outside. Several couples followed their lead and moved to the terrace. The same music drifted through the air as had thirty years ago, only this time it was pre-recorded rather than live. It appeared to be yet another lavish party at the Victorian mansion on Skull Island.

But there had been a slight change to the accuracy of the evening's activities from that party so long ago. As Henry VIII and Anne Boleyn danced back into the ballroom from the terrace, Gable and Lexi made their way through the darkness around the outside of the mansion to a hidden door leading directly into a secret stairway, leaving their doubles to remain on display for the next couple of hours.

They ascended the stairs to the third floor where they dumped their costumes in favor of jeans and dark sweaters. Lexi glanced around, a slight ripple of confusion catching her senses. "Where's Robert? Isn't he going with us?"

"Uncle Robert has some other last minute preparations to take care of." Gable pulled her into his arms. "Are you ready?"

Secrets—he still harbored secrets, something going on that he hadn't told her about. Something involving Robert. As much as her disappointment about his refusal to take her into his confidence settled inside her, she had to respect his integrity in keeping his word and standing behind his promise. She managed to muster a brave smile as she grabbed the flashlight. "As ready as I'll ever be."

Gable took the other flashlight, then they left the way they had come in. They quickly covered the ground between the mansion and the caretaker's cottage. After some consideration, Gable had changed his mind about searching the cottage. With Hank and Dolly busy in the kitchen helping the caterers, it provided the perfect time to search their living quarters for anything that proved they had knowledge of Winthrop Hollingsworth being alive all those years...something in addition to Hank's involvement in the original transfer of money to a Swiss bank account when Winthrop and Evelyn were still very much alive.

Lexi's first surprise was finding the doors of the cottage locked. Gable didn't keep the doors of his house locked, so why would Hank and Dolly feel the need to keep their doors locked? It was more than merely locked doors. Judging from Gable's quick flash of displeasure when he found his key didn't work, the locks had recently been changed. There certainly wasn't any type of a logical explanation for that. At least not an innocent one.

"Now what?" Even though there didn't seem to be any apparent reason to keep their voices low, she found herself whispering. "Do we break in?"

Gable's voice came out as a whisper no louder than hers had been. "I've got it covered." He produced a set of lock picks. A simple manipulation had them inside. He closed and locked the front door, leaving it just the way they had found it. She shot him a questioning look.

"Just in case. If Hank or Dolly have some sort of

emergency and need to return, I want the warning of hearing them unlock the door rather than turning around to find someone staring at me."

"No, I was questioning where you learned to pick locks."

His sheepish grin said it all. "A skill taught to me by my uncle Robert, the master illusionist."

They set about searching the cottage. Half an hour passed without finding anything suspicious. Then Lexi made a discovery. On the top shelf at the back of a closet hidden under a large folded comforter, she found a strong box. Not only was it locked, it had been wrapped with duct tape so the lid would not open without removing the tape. Any attempt to open the box would be readily noticeable. She carried it into the bathroom where Gable was searching the linen cupboard and handed it to him.

He pointed to the words written on the tape...*Evelyn and Winthrop Hollingsworth.* "That's Dolly's handwriting."

A rush of nervous energy swept through Lexi's body. Was this the proof they needed? Was Gable's long quest finally coming to an end? But to her surprise, he did not open the box. Instead he headed toward the front door. "Come on, we have to get this stashed away in a safe place."

"But aren't you going to open it?"

"No, not yet. I don't want to compromise whatever is in there by giving someone the availability of claiming I tampered with the contents, possibly planted something for the authorities to find."

She came to an abrupt halt, stopping him in his tracks. "Hide it where? If we go back to your house someone might see us, maybe one of the guards. It will be obvious that we haven't been at the party, especially since we're not even in costume."

"We'll hide it on the third floor of the mansion.

Déjà Vu

There's a small safe—"

A hard shot of adrenaline raced through Lexi's body followed by a cold shiver, a reaction that matched the look in Gable's eyes. Someone had rattled the doorknob on the front door.

He grabbed her hand, his voice carrying a real sense of urgency. "Damn...we've got to get out of here. Come on, the back door is our only option."

The sound of the lock being worked followed by the click of it opening told them they would never make it to the kitchen and out the back door without being detected. Her heart pounded and her mouth went dry as the adrenaline surged through her veins. The trepidation bordered on panic. Lexi looked to Gable for a decision. Anything to reassure her they would be safe.

Gable's response was decisive and immediate. He shoved her to the floor and then the two of them scooted under the bed. Lexi pulled in deep breaths as she tried to calm her escalating panic. She felt Gable's heart pound as he pressed his body against hers, covering her in a protective manner. She wasn't sure what to think. If it hadn't been such a dangerous situation it would almost have been weirdly surreal, as if it was a scene from a movie— the cheating wife and her lover being surprised by the husband who came home early, forcing them to hide in the only place they could find in a hurry.

But it wasn't a movie, she wasn't a cheating wife, and the consequences of being discovered could be deadly.

The sounds of drawers opening and closing and items being moved around filtered in from the living room. Lexi immediately recognized Brian's voice.

"Whatever it is you're looking for, we need to hurry. Hank or Dolly could come back here for something at any time."

"They're both occupied with the party."

Lexi didn't recognize the second voice. It seemed to be barking orders more than simply responding to Brian's concern. She shot a quick glance at Gable who seemed as mystified as she was about who the voice belonged to. They continued to listen.

"What is it you're looking for? Perhaps I can help you find it?"

"What I'm looking for, Brian, is my business! You keep a watch out the window for any unexpected visitors. I want you to keep an especially sharp lookout for Gable Talbot and Alexandra Caldwell."

"No need to worry there, Mr. Prescott. I confirmed that they're at the party, dancing in full view of all the guests. Besides, in those costumes they won't be doing much in the way of sneaking around."

The voices moved closer to the bedroom. Gable felt Lexi's grip tighten on his hand. A sharp adrenaline spike of excitement shot through his veins when he heard Brian call the second man by name. The voice was not the Prescott imposter. That meant only one thing. The man Brian addressed as Mr. Prescott was actually Winthrop Hollingsworth who had finally returned to the scene of the crime. After all these years Gable would be able to come face-to-face with the chief nemesis of his life, the man who had cold-bloodedly murdered two people and deprived him of a father with callous disregard for everything other than his own greed.

Gable's momentary excitement quickly turned to cold calculating thoughts. The next few hours would be critical. They would spell the difference between Winthrop merely being unmasked and them being able to prove he committed the murders. His thoughts jerked back to the present when the two men entered the bedroom. From beneath the bed he could see their feet, Brian's boots and uniform pants

Déjà Vu

and a pair of running shoes and jeans belonging to the other man.

Neither of the men spoke. Brian remained by the bedroom door as the other man walked around, opened dresser drawers, then finally opened the closet door. Gable listened as the other man moved things in the closet, then shut the door.

"Tell me, Brian. Is there some other place where either Hank or Dolly spend a considerable amount of their time?"

"Yes, sir, Mr. Prescott. Naturally Dolly spends a lot of time at Mr. Talbot's house. I've already apprised you of the situation with his office safe and computer. But Hank uses the carriage house behind the mansion as a work shop and a place where he stores various tools and gardening supplies. He's there several times a day and in bad weather he quite often works the entire day in the carriage house."

"Excellent. I want to make a quick check of the kitchen. If I don't find anything here, we'll go to the carriage house."

"Uh...I don't know, Mr. Prescott. With the party in full swing at the mansion, this might not be a good time for you to go poking around inside the carriage house with so many people close by."

Gable didn't hear the other man give any response to Brian's concerns. He watched Brian's boots move from the bedroom door back toward the living room. Before he could breathe a sigh of relief the other man's running shoes came to a halt only about two feet away. Then they turned toward the bed. He tightened his hold on Lexi, keeping her wrapped in the protection of his arms as he also held his breath. His heart pounded as the adrenaline pumped through his veins.

"We need to hurry, Mr. Prescott." Brian's voice called from the living room. "I'm due to check with

199

each of the guards and need to stay on schedule so no one gets suspicious."

The long pause seemed like it lasted forever, then the running shoes turned and walked toward the bedroom door. He heard the intruders move toward the kitchen. Another five minutes and the two men left the way they had come, through the front door. Gable continued to hold Lexi in place for several more minutes to make sure their adversaries wouldn't be coming back.

They finally emerged from beneath the bed. Gable brushed his fingertips across her cheek. "You okay?"

"My nerves are rattled, but everything else is all right." She quickly pulled herself together and collected her composure. "That was Winthrop Hollingsworth with Brian, wasn't it? I wonder how long he's been on the island and where he's been hiding?"

"I doubt he's been here very long, probably only a few hours. Brian knows the location of the security cameras, so was able to guide Hollingsworth from the cove without being detected. The only place Brian could hide him—other than sticking him up a tree somewhere—would be in his own personal quarters and he certainly couldn't keep him there for long if for no other reason than needing to feed him without anyone seeing Brian sneaking out food."

"I got the impression that Hank and Dolly don't know he's here and that he didn't want to run into them...at least not while he was with Brian."

"Yeah, same here. I think that pretty much confirms that Brian only knows him as J.D. Prescott and Hank and Dolly only know him as Winthrop Hollingsworth and he needs to keep that separate for his own protection. And that leaves him in a very precarious position, treading a thin line. My guess is that he was searching for any records Hank and

Dolly may have that would prove some of his manipulations with the money." Gable started toward the front door. "Come on, we need to get out of here. There's still work to be done before the big announcement moment tonight."

They hurried back to the mansion, again accessing the secret stairs to the third floor. Lexi watched as Gable opened the hidden safe in the small office area and put the box inside it. She blinked several times and straightened to attention when he removed a holster containing a 9mm semi-automatic hand gun and surreptitiously clipped it to his jeans under his sweater before closing the safe. The anxiety shivered through her body. But before she could say anything, the vision flashed in her mind again, striking without warning. She squeezed her eyes shut and stumbled backward a couple of steps. The image attacked her senses. So vivid. So real.

A hard jolt of fear shot through her at the same time as the vision she had seen before of the man firing the gun point blank at Gable. Her entire body trembled to the point where she couldn't control it. A sick churning knotted in the pit of her stomach. The single word came out as a frightened whisper.

"Gable..."

His arms circled around her, pulling her tightly into the comfort and security of his embrace, but alarm surrounded his words. "What is it, Lexi? What's wrong?"

She desperately tried to bring some semblance of calm to her voice. They were in the final stages of his plan. He needed to feel confident that he could depend on her without her strange visions interfering. Somehow she had to control them, or at least control her reactions to them.

"The vision, someone shooting at you." She squeezed her eyes tighter. "I can't see any background. I don't know where…"

"Don't worry." He brushed a soft kiss against her lips, then cradled her head against his shoulder. "Everything is going to be all right."

Then another vision assaulted her…a new one creating a new level of fear inside her. She wrapped her arms around his waist and buried her face against his chest. Someone running…the unstable ground giving way and dumping the person into the ravine…mud sliding into the ravine and burying someone. Who was this person? She couldn't tell if it was a man or a woman. Even though this vision of someone falling into the ravine and being buried by the mud was not from her point of view as the vision of the mud sliding toward her had been, her entire body shook as the cold wave crashed through her accompanied by the terrifying memory of what had happened.

The unwelcome psychic visions hadn't finished with her. Yet another vision, equally frightening. Two bodies, a man and a woman. She couldn't see any faces. The clothes they were wearing not clearly defined. Sprawled face down in the sand at the cove. Dead.

Someone being buried in a mud slide. Two dead bodies at the cove. New visions in addition to a repeat of the one with someone firing a gun at Gable. What the hell were they trying to tell her? How could she stop the events from happening? Hard spasms shuddered through her body as the fear coursed through her veins. But not fear for her own safety.

The words screamed inside her mind. *How can I protect Gable?*

She shoved away from his embrace. Somehow she had to shut off the frightening intrusions. Gable was depending on her to do her part. Her full attention had to be directed to the problem at

Déjà Vu

hand—bringing the rest of the plan to fruition. But how? If anything happened to him…

"Lexi, honey…what's wrong?" The alarm filled his voice. "You're trembling and you look like you've seen a ghost."

"It's…visions…images…" She sucked in a calming breath as she squared her shoulders and clenched her jaw in determination. She put as much control into her voice as she could muster. "It's nothing." She offered what she hoped looked like a confident smile. "Just a little nervous tension. We have work to do."

Even though she remained in the dark about several of the details of what was to transpire that night, she knew what he expected of her. She also knew Gable anticipated trouble. Or at the very least, had prepared himself in case something went wrong. There wasn't any other way to interpret the hand gun he took from the safe. And since he hadn't volunteered an explanation, she decided not to ask.

He placed a loving kiss on her lips. "It's almost over. Another hour or two and we can put this behind us." He glanced at his watch. "The Prescott imposter will be making his scheduled announcement in about ten minutes, then I make my surprise announcement which should force Winthrop out of hiding. Even though he has hired an actor to impersonate him, I have no doubts that he'll be somewhere close by so he can hear what I'm going to say in response to his imposter's announcement. That's when I'll draw him out into the open and we'll have him."

She couldn't keep the gravity of the situation out of her voice. "Be careful, Gable. This isn't a game. It's deadly serious and I don't want anything to happen to you."

He smiled at her, a smile that melted her heart. "When this is all over, we have things to talk about...important things. I promise I'm not going to let anything happen to me, especially with so much to look forward to."

He brushed another brief kiss against her mouth, then his manner became somber...the type of seriousness that left her very uneasy, as if waiting for the other shoe to drop. "But for now I need to have you do something for me. You're not going to like it, but it's very important."

She tried to swallow the anxiety that had suddenly invaded her awareness. That other shoe was about to drop. "Of course. I'll do anything you need."

Gable placed his hands on her shoulders, his face showing his nervous tension. "I *need* for you to stay here where you'll be safe."

His words caught her by surprise. "You want me to stay here on the third floor, tucked away from what's happening? What about the tasks you gave me to do...my part of the operation for tonight?"

"We don't need to have the electric carts disabled. They can't get anyone off the island. I've already stationed Ralph at the dock. The guard on duty at the security office has been stationed at the cove and he'll alert me to anyone in the vicinity, whether approaching the cove from the ocean or headed to the cove from the island. The thing you can do now that will help me the most is to stay here so I'll know you're safe."

An increased level of apprehension welled inside her. "But I want to help. And what about my vision...the one where someone is shooting at you—"

He placed his fingertips to her lips to stop her words. "I promise you, no one will shoot me. Now, I want you to promise me you'll stay here until I come and get you. Okay?"

"But I—"

"Please, Lexi...promise me you'll stay here

Déjà Vu

where you'll be safe."

She glanced down at the floor, then expelled a sigh of resignation. "Okay, I'll stay out of trouble."

"Nice try, but that isn't what I asked. Promise me you'll stay *here*."

She forced out a barely audible response. "Okay, I won't leave."

Gable gave her hand a reassuring squeeze, then returned to the hidden stairs. She watched him disappear behind the sliding panel. Lexi wasn't sure exactly what she felt. It seemed to be part anxiety, part irritation and part stubborn determination. *I promised not to leave the mansion, but that doesn't mean I won't leave the third floor.* Maybe Gable didn't take her visions seriously, but she did. She had no doubt that the vision she saw of a gun being fired at Gable foretold a very real incident. A very frightening incident. She had no intention of sitting there and letting it happen.

She could easily reach the ground floor from inside the mansion without using the secret stairs and being outside, so technically she wouldn't be breaking her promise to not leave. After all, she didn't specifically promise not to leave the third floor. She only promised not to leave. So, as long as she remained inside the mansion...

A little twinge of guilt told her she had drawn a very thin line.

The wide curved staircase from the ground floor went up to the second floor landing, then continued to the third floor with a door between the staircase and the third floor hallway. That door could be locked from the third floor side. It prevented someone from gaining access from the floors below...what could be construed as a private residence within the mansion...rather than keeping anyone from leaving the third floor to go downstairs.

And she knew just the place to hide where she

could keep an eye on the activities in the ballroom without anyone being able to see her.

And her previous explorations of the mansion told her how to get there without being spotted.

****

"Okay, Gable. Stand over here and we'll give this one last run through before…" Robert Stinson paused as he stared at his nephew for a second. "Not to change the subject, but what do you plan to do about your name when all of this is over? It's taken five years, but I've finally gotten use to calling you Gable. Are you going to have your name changed back to Jonathon Stinson?"

Gable wrinkled his brow in a moment's concentration. "I don't know. I haven't really given it any thought. I haven't been able to think beyond seeing Winthrop Hollingsworth in jail. Except for one thing…"

Robert cocked his head to the side and raised a questioning eyebrow. "And would that one thing be Alexandra Caldwell? Even a blind man can see the way you look at her and every time you mention her name that look comes into your eyes."

A moment of uncertainty accompanied his words. "It's that obvious?"

"It is to these eyes and they have exceptional vision."

Gable glanced at his watch and attempted to change the subject. "We don't have time to be discussing abstract things. The Prescott imposter will be making his announcement in ten minutes. Then it's my turn to draw Winthrop out of hiding."

He sucked in a deep breath, held it for several seconds, then slowly exhaled. *If this doesn't work…if Winthrop is on to us…if he doesn't take the bait*…Gable shook away the negative thoughts. There was no room or time for doubts.

Robert and Gable did a last minute check of the

Déjà Vu

equipment Robert had set up in the windowless room off the ballroom, a secured location where they could observe and control everything without anyone else having access to the locked room. In the prime days of the mansion parties, the room was used to store the musicians instruments and as a lounge where the band took their break.

As soon as Robert and Gable were satisfied that everything was ready, Gable spoke into the miniature earpieces worn by both his and Lexi's stand-ins in the ballroom.

"As we discussed, when I stop the music you ask for everyone to move to the sides of the dance floor, then call Prescott front and center to make his announcement. The assembled guests will most likely applaud his statement when he's finished. At that time when all attention is on him, the two of you slip out the side door and head straight for the dock. Ralph will hand you a check for your services and see that you're immediately transported back to the mainland. I thank you for your fine performance and remind you of the confidentiality agreement you signed preventing you from talking to anyone about this. I'll be stopping the music in five minutes, so get into position."

The stress surged just below the surface of Gable's skin. The next hour would be the most tense and stressful time he had ever endured. From the age of fifteen he had been working toward this moment with unwavering dedication. And now...just a little while longer and it would all be over. The culmination of twenty-five years of effort.

"This is it, lad." Robert hugged his nephew, a gesture immediately returned by Gable.

"Right you are, Uncle Robert."

Gable stopped the music, then watched through the viewing portal as his stand-in played out the part, including an excellent imitation of Gable's voice. It took only a couple of minutes for him to clear the dance floor and bring the Prescott imposter to the center of the ballroom to make his announcement.

Hal Bentley played the part of J.D. Prescott to perfection. "Ladies and gentlemen. I know your host, Gable Talbot, has already welcomed you, but I would like to extend my personal welcome and appreciation for this wonderful turnout tonight. This truly marvelous house...this gracious and magnificent ballroom...this must be just the way it looked that night thirty years ago when most of you were in attendance at another party.

"As has been reported, I'm using the disappearance of Winthrop and Evelyn Hollingsworth as the launching event for my next book, a story that does not follow the real life events but starts there. Several incidents have occurred in the last few days that shed new light on the mystery of what happened to Winthrop and Evelyn and also reinforce my solution to the decades-old mystery.

"As you are no doubt aware, two bodies...actually skeletons...were discovered a few days ago less than a hundred yards from here. They were naturally assumed to be Evelyn and Winthrop Hollingsworth. Evelyn's identity was immediately confirmed through dental records and it was dental records that ruled out the other skeleton being Winthrop. For those of you who aren't aware, it was my researcher, Alexandra Caldwell, who provided the authorities with a means of positively identifying the other skeleton as Jack Stinson, a Hollingsworth employee who went missing that same day.

"And then, to the shock of everyone connected with this matter, Gable Talbot came forth and admitted to being the son of Jack Stinson and provided the authorities with a DNA sample in order to reinforce the identification of his father and prove his own identity. The authorities have verified through court records showing a change of name that Mr. Talbot is who he claims to be. Miss Caldwell's presence on Skull Island was at my behest to provide me with some additional information, a situation that ultimately put her in extreme danger."

Hal Bentley worked his audience as if it was opening night on Broadway, making sure he had everyone in the room totally engaged and hanging on his every word. "I encouraged Mr. Talbot to host this party prior to the disclosure of his true identity. My purpose was to present you with my well researched and carefully constructed solution to the thirty year old mystery. The unexpected events that have occurred in the last few days only go to reinforce my belief that my solution is the only possible one and finally closes this case after all these years."

The stand-ins for Gable and Lexi eased their way toward the side door as they had been instructed. They moved slowly and carefully, pausing every few steps to make sure there wasn't anyone watching them. Lexi's stand-in reached for her mask as if to remove it, but Gable's stand-in quickly stopped her.

Hal Bentley continued with his rehearsed performance. "So, I'll cut to the chase and give you the solution to the mystery, including what happened to Winthrop Hollingsworth who, it turns out, was not buried here on the island he owned." He paused for a moment, more for dramatic effect than anything else. "It was Winthrop Hollingsworth who murdered his wife, Evelyn. Then he murdered Jack Stinson, an employee, in order to have a scapegoat for his crime." He paused again as a collective gasp came from the assembled party guests.

"The inevitable conclusion, the one Winthrop

wanted, said that Jack Stinson had murdered both Evelyn and Winthrop and escaped that same night. Winthrop believed the authorities would accept that theory as fact and the case would be put on the back shelf to languish. Well, the case did end up on that shelf, but not before one more murder and then years later another death occurred both connected to the original crime of thirty years ago.

"Jack was shot before the party and his body hidden away in the carriage house. During the power outage that Winthrop staged, he shot Evelyn and put her body with Jack's. He buried them later that night, with the storm as his ally in obscuring the freshly dug grave. Then the murderer prepared to make his escape, to steal away under cover of that same storm without anyone seeing him.

"Now…at this time I'd like to introduce you to a new player in our little drama." He opened the long cardboard tube he had in his hand, extracted a poster, unrolled it and held it up for everyone to see. "This, ladies and gentlemen, is Santorini The Great, known the world over as a master illusionist. In real life, Robert Stinson—Jack Stinson's twin brother. Brothers are close. Sisters are close. But twins are so close that they are almost like one. Robert retired from performing two years ago. I tracked him down in Spain and interviewed him about the night his brother disappeared. The story he related to me is truly amazing and I want to share it with you now." An excited murmur ran through the assembled guests, showing that he had their undivided attention.

"According to Robert, he had been on the island that night to meet with his brother, unknown to anyone else. But his brother did not appear at the designated location. Robert remained out of sight and later that night he witnessed Winthrop murder Evelyn. That's when he located his brother, when

Déjà Vu

Winthrop hid his wife's body with the body of the already dead Jack Stinson. Robert feared no one would believe him with it being his word against someone as powerful as Winthrop Hollingsworth. And, you have to remember, those were the days before DNA and all the high tech forensic tools available to today's investigators.

"Robert continued to watch Winthrop and saw him bury the bodies. His grief at the death of his twin brother caused him to confront the murderer. They struggled and Winthrop ended up shot with his own gun. Now Robert was really in a quandary. He took Winthrop's body and left the island the way Winthrop had planned to escape, using the small boat hidden away in the cove...the boat employees reported as having disappeared that night. Robert dumped Winthrop's body at sea, then returned to his touring schedule and spent the next few years performing out of the country. Robert Stinson, unfortunately, perished in an automobile accident in Spain shortly after I interviewed him."

The Gable and Lexi stand-ins slipped out the side door and headed toward the dock as Hal Bentley finished his J.D. Prescott performance. "That, ladies and gentlemen, is what happened here that night thirty years ago. With the death of Robert Stinson there isn't anyone alive who had a connection to the disappearances. And that closes the case. I will be happy to turn over copies of my notes of the interview with Robert Stinson to the authorities to be placed in the official file as corroborating evidence.

"And now Gable Talbot would like to make a statement." The Prescott imposter scanned the assembled faces. A slight frown wrinkled across his forehead when he didn't see Gable anywhere. "Mr. Talbot? Are you here?" Then the voice intruded from the far side of the ballroom.

"I'm afraid I'm going to have to disagree with Mr. Prescott's summation."

Everyone turned toward the sound to be greeted by the sight of Gable Talbot standing on the bandstand dressed in jeans and a sweater. The look of total confusion on the face of the Prescott imposter was the response Gable wanted. His internal nervousness subsided and a calm settled over him as he continued to talk.

"First I'd like to introduce you to this man." Gable gestured toward the Prescott imposter. "This is not J.D. Prescott. This man is an actor named Hal Bentley." He addressed his comment directly to the imposter. "I'm sure if there was a critic here, you'd have an excellent review for this performance. But for now, I'd appreciate it if you'd take a seat over there against the wall because I'm sure the sheriff's department will be wanting to talk to you about your part in all of this."

Not a sound emanated from the assembled guests. The expressions on the collective faces said they were captivated by the strange turn of events unfolding in front of them and what Gable was saying. He had their total and complete attention. "Why, you are probably asking, would J.D. Prescott hire an actor to impersonate him? It's a well-known fact that he's a recluse, but to hire an actor to attend a party held on a private island with no access for the general public...a party being held at his insistence...well, that certainly needs a bit of explanation. And, as it happens, I have the answer to that question. J.D. Prescott could not risk appearing here in person. Even though it was thirty years ago, he could not take a chance on some of you recognizing him even if he wore a costume."

Excited voices again filtered through the air. Gable raised his hand. "Please hold your comments. I haven't finished with my little announcement yet."

Déjà Vu

He attempted to stop the slight grin turning the corners of his mouth, but without much success. "Let me assure you, ladies and gentlemen, the best is yet to come. First, let's tackle the question that is probably foremost in your mind and that would be exactly who is J.D. Prescott that he would be concerned about being recognized by the guests gathered here."

Gable looked toward Hal Bentley. "Perhaps our actor can shed some light on the situation. How about that, Hal?"

Gable hadn't planned on dragging things out, but the thought amused him of Winthrop hiding somewhere on the premises, watching and sweating out this unexpected intrusion into the drama he thought he had carefully orchestrated. Gable also wanted to do everything possible to aggravate Winthrop's panic at having lost control of his own carefully planned out drama. Hopefully Gable's nemesis would be forced into an impulsive and unwise course of action.

Hal's smooth performance totally collapsed. "I...I don't know what you're talking about."

The sarcasm dripped from Gable's words. "Of course not." He returned his attention to the assembled guests. "The only thing our fake Prescott had right was his statement that Winthrop killed his wife and my father. Any similarity to the truth stops at that point. J.D. Prescott is, in real life, none other than the missing but very much alive Winthrop Hollingsworth. And I have the proof."

A hushed silence fell over the room. Stunned expressions covered all the faces. Gable stood perfectly still, as if waiting for something to happen. And he didn't have to wait long.

A serving cart crashed to the floor, breaking the eerie silence. The man emerged from behind the drape in back of the cart. Anger colored his sixty-five-year-old face a bright red. His voice carried all the fury that contorted his features.

"You bastard! You won't get away with this slander. There is no proof—"

"My name is Jack Stinson and you, Winthrop Hollingsworth, shot me." The voice came from the man who had seemingly stepped from the shadows and stood next to Gable. "You murdered me just as you murdered your wife thirty years ago. And now I intend to make you pay for your crimes."

"NO!" Winthrop's anguished cry filled the room. The genuine look of fear covering his face far surpassed anything J.D. Prescott had ever written in his books. The man whose mind had created so many horror novels found himself on the receiving end of that terror. "You can't be Jack Stinson. This is a trick. A lie."

Winthrop yanked a gun from his pocket. His voice seethed with rage. "I killed you thirty years ago and I can do it again! Both of you!" In a state of frenzied panic, he fired point blank at both men. The party guests screamed and dove for cover, getting as far away from the scene as they could. He continued to squeeze the trigger until all the bullets had been spent. Yet both men remained standing, apparently unscathed by the brutal attack as the bullets passed through their bodies and lodged in the wall behind them.

And a horrified Winthrop Hollingsworth let out a blood curdling scream.

Déjà Vu

Chapter Thirteen

Absolute panic unlike anything she had ever known gripped Lexi's body and consciousness, engulfing her entire existence as she watched the man pointing the gun at Gable and Robert. The breath froze in her lungs and her mouth went dry. Hard tremors of fear bombarded her. A sick lump pushed its way up her throat, threatening to choke her if she couldn't find a way of stopping it.

But none of that mattered. The only reality she could comprehend was someone pointing a gun at Gable at point blank range—exactly like her vision. She bolted out of the closet and charged across the ballroom toward Gable. But before she could reach him, the shots rang out...one after the other. She heard screaming, then realized it had come from her.

"Gable...Gable...look out!" Her attention remained focused on Gable, even as she bumped into Winthrop and sent him stumbling sideways. Then, to her shock, both Gable and Robert disappeared right before her eyes. She came to an abrupt halt. The spot where they stood was now empty. Had she lost her mind? What happened?

The small door next to the bandstand opened. Gable and Robert emerged from the band room. Robert shoved his way through the crowd toward Winthrop and Gable reached for Lexi. "It's okay, Lexi. I'm fine. No one has been hurt."

She glanced over toward Winthrop struggling with Robert while the party guests slowly emerged from their hiding places, seemingly too stunned to know what to do. He plopped Lexi down into a chair.

"Stay here. I need to help Uncle Robert."

Lexi watched in stunned silence as Gable charged through the crowd. By the time he reached Robert, Winthrop broke free and ran out the ballroom door into the night. Gable paused long enough to make sure Robert wasn't hurt, then he gave chase after Winthrop.

"Gable!" Lexi called after him, but he disappeared into the darkness. She jumped up from the chair only to have Robert restrain her.

"Stay here, Lexi. It's not going to help Gable if he has to worry about you."

As much as she didn't like hearing it, she knew Robert was right. She would be a distraction and Gable needed to have all his wits and attention focused on Winthrop. Then another more important possibility hit her. What if Gable took out his vengeance on Winthrop? She had to keep him from doing something in a fit of long repressed anger that he would never do under normal circumstances.

****

Gable flashed on a quick thought about where Brian was as he dug his shoes into the soft ground to gain traction. Could he be waiting for Winthrop, ready with a boat to make a getaway as a back-up plan if something went wrong? Well, nothing could have gone more wrong for Hollingsworth than his confession in full view a room full of prominent people.

Another thought shot through Gable's mind as he raced through the night to catch up with his quarry. Winthrop disappeared from this same house thirty years ago and he had the money to do it again. A fierce anger spurred him on. No way would he allow Winthrop Hollingsworth to vanish again. He would do whatever it took to see that Winthrop did not get off the island any way other than being in

Déjà Vu

custody. He touched the 9mm snugged securely in the clip-on holster beneath his sweater at his waist, reassured by its presence.

No matter what it took.

The full moon illuminated the form of a man running along the path way out in front of him. A potent surge of adrenaline jolted through his body. He pumped his legs harder forcing himself into a faster pace. His heart pounded in his chest as he closed the distance between himself and his life long nemesis.

"Gable...be careful." Lexi's voice reached out to him. He slowed and glanced back over his shoulder.

"Robert has alerted the sheriff. Hollingsworth can't get off the island." Her words restored his logic and senses, bringing him to a halt.

"Lexi..." he whispered her name. Just the thought of having her in his arms allowed a sense of calm to settle over him. She was right. Winthrop couldn't get off the island, certainly not without help, and he had a guard stationed at the only two places where someone could reach a boat.

Millions of thoughts and feelings swirled around inside him, each screaming the same thing at him. Each telling him not to exchange his entire future...a future he hoped would include Lexi...for one moment of revenge-fueled satisfaction. One foolish act of vengeance could not change the past. Nothing would bring back his father and to end up disgracing his father's name was untenable.

Gable held his arms out to Lexi. A second later he had her wrapped in his embrace, her body pulled tightly against his. And nothing had ever provided him a greater sense of contentment. He felt her tremble and her heart pound as she caught her breath. And he continued to hold her.

Then a new sound filled the air. A man's scream followed by the rumble of moving earth. Gable and

Lexi advanced cautiously toward the sound. He took the flashlight from her and switched it on, then illuminated the path in front of them. The beam of light caught the bright yellow crime scene tape still cordoning off the area where the skeletons had been found.

Another sound grabbed their attention from behind, footsteps hitting the ground hard. Could it be Brian? Gable moved Lexi protectively behind him as he swung the flashlight beam around. It caught Robert running toward them. He turned it back in the direction Winthrop had gone. The scream, the rumble of moving earth, the unstable ground along the path. He could see in Lexi's eyes the identical realization that hit him. Winthrop had been caught in the same trap that had unearthed his victims.

As soon as Robert reached them, they cautiously made their way around the cordoned off area as quickly as they dared, keeping well away from the edge. When they reached the other side, Gable shined the light along the ravine and saw where the new slide had occurred. When they didn't see anything else, he tried again moving the beam of light slowly along the same area.

The light finally picked up something. A running shoe sticking out of the loose dirt. A running shoe identical to the one he had seen when hiding under the bed in Hank and Dolly's cottage.

Gable shoved his cell phone at Lexi, his voice filled with the urgency of the situation. "Winthrop can still be alive. Call Bud. We need a rescue crew."

Gable and Robert ignored the safety factors and jumped into the ravine. Gable's words came out in a raspy anger. "You're not going to escape your retribution by dying, you bastard. You'll pay for your crimes."

Using their hands, they frantically dug and scooped the mud away in a desperate attempt to pull

Winthrop free. An arm, then another arm. A moment later they had his head uncovered. Robert cleared the mud from his mouth and nose as Gable pulled him from the hole. They worked on him and a minute later had their efforts rewarded when Winthrop sputtered and choked as he gasped for air.

Gable stared at his long time nemesis. Winthrop Hollingsworth finally unmasked, exposed to the world as the ruthless killer he was. Twenty-five years of work and planning had come down to this moment. An arrogant bastard who didn't care about anything other than himself and his money, cowering on the ground covered in mud. Looking like a homeless unfortunate deserving of sympathy rather than the hated man worth millions who did not deserve anyone's sympathy.

Lexi's voice sounded less than firm. "My first vision, someone shooting at you. And now my second vision, someone being trapped by another mud slide. Both visions have come to fruition. But there's still the third one...a man and a woman face down on the sand at the cove...apparently dead."

"I can explain that one." Deputy Lansing walked up behind them accompanied by another deputy and a paramedic. The paramedic rushed ahead to check Winthrop.

"One of my men found your guard unconscious by the cove."

"Is he all right?" Gable's alarm and concern clearly showed in his voice.

"He took a nasty blow to the back of his head, but he's fine...a headache and a couple of stitches. We took Brian into custody at the cove. He had a boat and seemed to be waiting for someone." Bud gestured toward the mud spattered man on the ground. "I assume that someone is the guest of honor over there."

Lexi's voice cut into the conversation. "But what

about the man and woman face down in the sand? What I saw in my vision?"

Bud glanced down at the ground for a moment then looked up at Lexi before addressing Gable. "Hank and Dolly. They had been shot. My guess is that ballistics will match the bullets to Brian's weapon."

Confusion covered Lexi's face. "But why would Brian kill Hank and Dolly?"

Gable slipped his arm around her shoulder. "I think it had to do with what Winthrop was looking for in their cottage and that something is probably in the box we took from the closet."

Bud cocked his head, shot a quick glance at Robert, then leveled a questioning look at Gable. "Box? I thought we brought all your little secrets out in the open when we had our talk?"

"Lexi and I just found the box a little while ago. Right after we started the dancing in the ballroom, we ducked out of the party and left our stand-ins there as the visible presence while we searched Hank and Dolly's cottage."

The paramedic and deputy approached with a hand-cuffed Winthrop Hollingsworth in tow. The deputy addressed his comments to Bud Lansing. "He's lucky to be alive. Another minute or so under that mud and he would have been dead. But, as you can see, he's ambulatory and he'll be okay."

"Have the doctor check him out, then book him. For right now it's trespassing on private property, carrying a concealed weapon, and endangering others by firing that weapon inside a crowded room. The D.A. will be filing far more serious charges tomorrow." He glanced toward Winthrop. "There's no statute of limitations on murder."

Gable and Lexi watched as the deputy and paramedic escorted Winthrop to the dock and the waiting sheriff's launch. Then Gable turned toward

Déjà Vu

Bud. "Come on, I'll get that box for you."

They returned to the mansion, now abuzz with deputies taking statements from the party guests and crime scene personnel collecting evidence. Gable directed Bud around the outside of the mansion to the secret staircase so they could avoid the ground floor, followed by Lexi and Robert.

Gable removed the box from the safe and set it on the desk. He handed Bud a pair of scissors, then watched as the deputy cut away the tape and opened the lid. He withdrew a diary. Gable identified the entries as being in Dolly's handwriting. The box also contained some personal items tagged as belonging to Winthrop. Bud checked a few random pages of the diary.

"It appears that Dolly kept a record of everything Winthrop asked them to do including details of the money transfer. I'm sure the D.A. will find this very helpful." Bud replaced the diary and picked up the box. "I'll expect the three of you at the station in the morning," he glanced at his watch, "make that later today to make an official statement."

Gable noted Lexi and Robert nodding their agreement. "No problem."

"Now, just one little thing before I go. How did Winthrop fire all those shots at the two of you point blank and not hit either one of you? And according to witnesses, neither one of you even made an attempt to dive for cover. So, what gives?"

Robert stepped in to address Bud's question. "Deputy Lansing, a magician never reveals the secrets of his grand illusions. I'm afraid that's one thing that won't be going into your report."

"That's not good enough. I have to say something. My report can't simply say *several shots were seen to pass harmlessly through the two individuals and lodge in the wall behind them*. The sheriff isn't going to buy that for a second and neither will the district attorney."

Robert furrowed his brow in a moment of concentration. "Then tell them it was a carefully staged illusion by Santorini The Great utilizing the finest features of the art of holographic projection."

Bud let out a sigh of resignation, closed his notebook, and capped his pen. "I'll see if I can sell that to the powers that be."

Lexi stared at Gable for several seconds as if trying to get her mind wrapped around everything that happened in the last few hours. "Then you really weren't in any danger?"

"I told you I would be all right." He gave her hand an intimate little squeeze. "And I also think I told you to stay put on the third floor."

"Well...you didn't say exactly where I was supposed to stay, so I decided as long as I was still inside the mansion..." Her voice trailed off as she stared at Gable, her face covered in confusion.

Gable took her hand and stood quietly for a moment, then finally looked up. His voice carried all the emotion coursing through his veins. His gaze lit on Bud for a second, then settled on Robert Stinson. "It's over, Uncle Robert. It's finally over. This has been a large part of my life, my major focus, for twenty-five years. And I know for you it's been a very long thirty year odyssey."

Robert shot his nephew a big smile as he flashed a thumbs up gesture. "Well, it seems to me that you two kids have things to talk about. So, I think I'm going to go forth into the world and create my greatest illusion of all time. I'm going to return from the dead." He gave a wink to Lexi, clamped his hand affectionately on Gable's shoulder for a second, then headed down the hall toward the room where he had been staying.

After another five minutes of dealing with some

loose ends, Bud released Gable and Lexi from the scene until the next morning when they were to make an official statement at the sheriff's station. Bud assured Gable he'd see that the party guests were transported back to the mainland. His men would stay with the catering people until they had everything cleaned up, then take them to the mainland while leaving a couple of deputies on duty at the dock to thwart any trespassers.

Gable held onto Lexi's hand as they walked back to his house. She wasn't sure exactly what to say. He seemed so deep in thought that she was almost afraid to intrude and invade his privacy. "Bud and his men sure got here in a hurry."

"They were already here. Their launch docked right after all the party guests were taken to the mansion. They waited at the dock for a call."

She studied his expression for a moment, not quite sure what to make of it. It seemed to be an odd combination of anguish and relief. "I'm so sorry about Hank and Dolly. That didn't need to happen. Hollingsworth murdered two people thirty years ago and then had two more people killed tonight in an attempt to preserve his secret."

"Finally...there's nothing left but the details. We'll give our statements and then I'm sure there will be a round of questions from the D.A.'s office and most likely from Winthrop's defense attorney, too, which means I need to get my attorney involved. It will eventually go to trial. I think the evidence is overwhelming. He made a confession to killing my father in front of a room full of people, many of them prominent business leaders and even a couple of politicians. He also tried to kill Uncle Robert and me in front of those same witnesses. His attorney will probably go for an insanity plea. But the most important aspect of all of this is over. Winthrop Hollingsworth has been unmasked and will be held accountable. My father's name has been cleared. All the rest is just after-the-fact details."

They reached the house and went directly to Gable's bedroom. He leaned back against the closed door. His voice was soft, again filled with an emotion that touched her on every level. "It's over. It's really over. Somehow I thought it would feel like a huge weight being lifted from my shoulders. An overwhelming sensation of joy. I thought finally seeing that bastard exposed for the murderer he is would fill that empty void inside me that I've been carrying around for twenty-five years. But the truth is..." He caught a moment of eye contact with her, his gaze feeling as if it was trying to delve into the depths of her soul. "The truth is that I don't know how I feel or what I feel. I'm numb inside."

She touched her fingers to his cheek, gently caressing his skin. "So much has happened in the last couple of hours. You need time to come down from the adrenaline surge, time to emotionally assimilate all of it. Things will be much clearer in the morning after you've had a good night's sleep."

"Yeah, I'm sure you're right." He pulled her into his arms and held her close as he threaded his fingers through her hair. "But all I want right now is to shut out the rest of the world."

Lexi's heart pounded and her pulse raced...a combination of excitement and anticipation, yet it was somehow tinged with a hint of anxiety. Another psychic warning or her own insecurities playing havoc with her emotions? One thing for sure, her research job had come to a screeching halt and it was a good bet that J.D. Prescott wouldn't be paying her.

She had known all along that the time would come when she needed to return to real life, to leave Skull Island and once again embrace the necessity of job hunting and earning a living. But somehow she had missed the possibility of everything abruptly coming to such a quick conclusion. Could she honestly expect Gable to suddenly declare his undying love for her? And exactly what were her feelings toward him? Had she truly fallen in love with him in such a short time? Even though everything they had shared was more than many people experience in a lifetime, it had been less than a week since her arrival on the island. Was it even possible to fall in love that quickly?

Her troubling thoughts vanished in a flash of heated desire when he scooped her up in his arms and carried her to his bed.

They made love with all the passion two people could possess followed by all the tenderness two people could share. Physically satisfying...absolutely. Gable was the most incredible lover she had ever experienced. Emotionally satisfying...she didn't know. She didn't seem to be able to unravel the intricacies of the emotions coursing through her. If only she knew what he wanted.

She remained folded in the security of his arms, neither of them moving or speaking. Thoughts...fears...desires...uncertainties. Everything swirled around in her mind until exhaustion finally claimed her and she drifted into an uneasy sleep.

****

Gable stared at his reflection in the bathroom mirror until the steam from the shower obscured the image. He had never felt so completely lost and it wasn't due only to the fact that the primary focus of all his energy for the last twenty-five years no longer existed. When Lexi had returned to her room at sunrise saying she needed to pack, it had thrown him for a loop. The possibility of her leaving the island so soon...in fact, her leaving at all...hadn't sunk into his consciousness yet. He understood her reasons, her need to get back to work to earn a living, not wanting to be away from her home any longer than need be. Yes, he understood it intellectually. But emotionally? He didn't understand any of it.

So why had he allowed her to walk out of his bedroom and disappear down the hall? Why didn't he go after her? He suddenly felt like a ship adrift at sea. No wind to fill his sails. No navigational charts to show him what course to follow. No rudder to steer him in the proper direction.

Lexi was all those things. She was his life. But how to tell her? What to say?

He dressed and went to the kitchen to make coffee. One thing for sure, she couldn't leave until she had given her statement to Bud at the Sheriff's station. That would buy him some time, but not much.

"Well, I'm packed...except for my computer stuff in your office."

He whirled around at the sound of her voice. "I've made coffee. What would you like for breakfast?" *You stupid jerk. You couldn't think of anything more clever to say than that?* He hadn't known what else to say. Somehow he needed to find the right words to adequately express the feelings swirling around inside him.

"I'm not very hungry. I thought I'd give my official statement to Bud this morning and make sure he has my contact information before I head for home..."

"Head for home?" He couldn't keep the anxiety out of his voice. "You've already made plane reservations?"

"Uh...yes. I called first thing this morning. I can get a flight out of Seattle late this afternoon." *But I don't want to go.* She swallowed the sob that tried to form. It felt as if her entire world was being yanked out from beneath her, but she didn't know what else

Déjà Vu

to do. *I don't want to ever leave.*

She saw the panic dart through his eyes. A little flicker of hope burst to life deep inside her.

"Do you suppose you could delay your departure?"

"Delay it?" Could it be? Her breath caught in her lungs. Was it possible? Was he trying to say...

"We...uh...we need to talk."

"About what?" She had barely been able to force out the words. It seemed that her entire life...her entire future... had become dependent on what he was trying to say.

"About us...about the future."

His words touched the depths of her soul. Nothing had ever sounded so good. She blinked back the tears and prayed she wasn't misinterpreting what he had said.

He slowly reached out toward her, gently brushed his fingertips across her cheek, then pulled her into his arms. His voice sounded hesitant, as if he wasn't sure of what he wanted to say or how to say it. "For twenty-five years my life has been dedicated to one purpose. Last night, all of that came to a crashing halt. I found myself without any direction and it frightened me. You told me I needed time to assimilate everything that had happened. Well...you were right. This morning it all looks different to me. I'm not sure what the future holds or what I'll be doing, but one thing is crystal clear to me. I want you to be part of that future...part of my life."

He paused, as if trying to gather his thoughts. "What I'm trying to say is that I don't want you to leave."

Had she heard him correctly? Did she dare to hope? "You...you want me to stay?"

He slowly shook his head. "I'm making a complete mess out of this, but it's an area where I

227

haven't had any experience. I know this is sudden and it's been a time fraught with turmoil and complications, but I...I don't want to lose you."

He brushed a soft kiss across her lips. His words came out as a mere whisper, but there was no mistaking the emotion attached to them. "I love you, Lexi."

He was right. It had all happened so quickly and definitely under very adverse circumstances. But she had never heard more glorious words in her life. "Are you sure? You're not saying that just because you think it's what I want to hear, are you?"

"I'm saying it because I can't imagine my life without you. Please stay."

"Oh, Gable..."

He leaned back far enough to make eye contract with her. "Is that a yes?"

"Yes! Oh, yes...yes...yes!"

"Would I be pushing my luck if I took it one step farther?"

"What do you mean?"

"I don't have a ring to give you, but...uh...will...will you marry me?"

"Marry you? Did I hear you right?"

"Yes. Alexandra Caldwell, will you do me the honor of becoming my wife?"

Tears of joy trickled down her cheeks. "I love you, Gable." She had never been so sure of anything in her entire life as she was at that moment. "Oh, of course I'll marry you."

About the author...

Samantha Gentry currently lives in Kansas, but has lived most of her life in the Los Angeles area. She has fond hopes of being able to move back to the West Coast. For twenty years she worked in television production before becoming a full time writer.

For many years photography was her avocation. Research showed that she had a better chance of marketing her photographs to magazines if they included an article, so that's when and how she started writing non-fiction magazine articles to accompany her photographs.

She found that she thoroughly enjoyed the writing process. The magazine articles eventually segued into writing fiction and novels. In late 2005, after having twenty novels published by Harlequin/Silhouette under the pseudonym of Shawna Delacorte, she discovered ebooks and had her first ebook published in January 2006. Samantha continues to write for Harlequin in addition to publishing ebooks.

For the last nine years she has taught an eight-week fiction writing class twice a year at the university.

Samantha loves to travel and has been to England/UK several times.

Visit Samantha at www.samanthagentry.com

Thank you for purchasing
this Wild Rose Press publication.
For other wonderful stories of romance,
please visit our on-line bookstore at
www.thewildrosepress.com

For questions or more information,
contact us at
info@thewildrosepress.com

The Wild Rose Press
www.TheWildRosePress.com

Other suspense-filled Roses to enjoy
from The Wild Rose Press

DON'T CALL ME DARLIN' by Fleeta Cunningham. Texas, 1957: Carole faces not only censorship but mysterious threats and a fire-setting assailant. Will the County Judge who's dating her protect or accuse her?

~from Vintage Rose (historical 1900s)

SECRETS IN THE SHADOWS by Sheridon Smythe. Lovely widow Lacy had taken in two young children—and the rambunctious little angels wasted no time getting her into trouble with Shadow City's new sheriff...

~from Cactus Rose (historical Western)

SOLDIER FOR LOVE by Brenda Gale—An award-winning novel set on a lush Caribbean island. As CO of the American peacekeeping force, Julie has her hands full dealing with voodoo signs and a handsome subordinate.

~from Last Rose of Summer (older heroines)

TASMANIAN RAINBOW by Pinkie Paranya. A concert violinist grapples with remote ranch life, intrigue and the mystery of a missing diary, the peril of a flood in which all could be lost, and the undeniable attraction of the man who would do anything to protect his son.

~from Champagne Rose (contemporary)

THAT MONTANA SUMMER by Sloan Seymour. Samantha has everything but love. Dalton has only one thing on his mind: land. Neither wants to be a summer fling or be stalked by a mysterious attacker.

~from Yellow Rose (contemporary Western)

A CHANGE OF HEART by Marianne Arkins. Jake Langley returns to Wyoming to find more than changes at the family ranch. Discovery of a well-kept secret sets duty against heart's desire, changing hearts and lives forever.

~from Yellow Rose (contemporary Western)

DRAKE'S RETREAT, by Wendy Davy. Maggie needs a place to hide. Drake's Retreat, deep in the Sierra Nevada Mountains, is the perfect solution. But she has to convince the intimidating resort owner to let her stay.

~from White Rose (inspirational)